RETALIATE

SIN CITY OUTLAWS BOOK THREE

M. N. FORGY

RETALIATE

Edited by Ellie McLove
Cover Photography Sara Eirew
Proofed by Kim Ginsberg
Formatted by Max Henry

This book in no way displays the law enforcement in Las Vegas, though there are details that are accurate it wouldn't be any fun if we didn't twist it with some fiction.

A past never told to the innocent,

until whispered by the convict.

PROLOGUE

BROWN 5

Age unknown

My ribs hurt and my head is pounding. I'm so cold my teeth are starting to chatter. I'm in the far side of my cage where the light – a naked light bulb hangs from the ceiling of the corridor- doesn't reach. I want to sleep, but that's when the rats get you. Pulling my finger up I inspect the cut on my thumb from the rat that bit me last night when I was sleeping.

Scooting across the dirt floor, I pull my bloody matted hair away from my face and rest my head on the metal bars that contain me in my cage. I can hear a girl crying across from me. I don't cry anymore, it doesn't help you none. It just seems to piss the handlers off and dehydrate you. Seeing as we don't get food or water very much, it seems like a waste to cry over something that won't change. Flies land and fly around the bucket behind me, which is where I use the bathroom when needed and hasn't been dumped in days. My stomach cramps with a loud growl and I hunch over in pain. I lost my last fight and haven't eaten in days, and I need a bath. I should have tried harder, but I hate hurting other people. Especially Black A. She has dark hair and the saddest eyes I've ever seen. She is skinny from not eating, and weak. Digging my toes into the dirt floor, I wonder what awaits me when I'm next taken out of my cage. Will I fight again? Or will I be instructed to shoot that gun again? I hate the gun, it's too big for my hands.

Sighing, my head falls to my knees, and I begin to a draw the sun into the mud with my fingernail. I can't help but wonder what the purpose of all this is. Why am I here, and what they want with me? I stopped thinking about my parents a long time ago. I don't remember their faces, and like someone who died you begin to slowly forget even if you don't want to.

I was so excited to see the M&M store that day. Closing my eyes, I remember getting pulled back in the crowd of people on the sidewalk, then a cloth shoved over my face. Black took over my fear before I could scream, and I woke up here.

That was a long time ago though.

"Brown 5, up!" Black Hat snaps me from my blurred memory. That's what I call him as I don't know his name and he's always wearing a black hat. I asked him his name once and he got so mad I was put on a leash. I'm also not allowed to look him straight in the eye but I sometimes sneak a glimpse when his hat is pulled up just a little. He has dark beady eyes and tanned skin. It makes me jealous to think he gets to play in the sun as much as he wants while I only get to see it when I'm brought out to train. Black Hat is my caregiver and trainer. There is someone higher than him, but I've never met him. I just know all this is for him. That he is preparing for a war and we are his soldiers.

"I said up, Brown 5!" Black Hat snaps, slamming a metal baseball bat against the cage. The sound of metal against metal makes my ears ring.

I stand on shaky legs and await my next command. Looking

under my thick lashes, I wonder what it would be like to kill Black Hat. Let him see what it's like to fight for his life. Quickly I look down, scared he can read my thoughts and I'll be punished.

"You'll be training with an opponent today, so turn around." Black Hat twirls his finger indicating he wants me to turn around, so I do.

"Who am I fighting today?" I ask with a scratchy voice, wanting water so bad it hurts. He ignores me, and fists my mud-plastered hair, braiding it. "You got this one Brown 5," he whispers as his fingers make quick work of my dark hair. I bite my bottom lip to not smile, but it's useless. Black Hat is fond of me - or I like to think so anyway. He thinks I have potential to make the Boss happy and I long for that approval.

Following Black Hat, we pass the other rooms - cages. Girls and boys pull and tug on the barred doors, screaming and yelling for food and water. The sound used to bother me, but now I find it to be soothing - like a lullaby. If I don't hear it, I can't sleep at night. I need to hear the fear and terror in their screams. It drowns out my own despair.

I follow him down the dirt tunnel where the coldness that usually bites into your bones begins to dissipate into something much warmer. We must be closer to the surface, to the desert floor. We are underground, I know that much, the only escape I know of is the big break in the dirt ceiling where we battle one another.

Sunshine illuminates just down the path, and my feet begin to pick up the pace in excitement. I want to feel the rays of sunshine, feel its warmth on my skin. They tell you hell is a hot place filled with fire and terror, but I'm here to tell you it's dark and freezing cold.

"Easy, Brown 5," Black Hat warns, and I slow my pace. At

the end of the tunnel, it opens to a wide circle. The ceiling opened to a bright blue sky. I walk into the sun splayed along the blood-splattered ground, and lean my head back, soaking in the heat. It feels so good, so warm I close my eyes and inhale the fresh smell, the slight breeze that swirls down from above.

A fist to the back of my head snaps me into the moment. Pain racing through my skull and pounding behind my eyes until they water. My brows furrowing, and heart beating hard I turn with a high kick to whoever my opponent is.

It's Black A. Her hair is cut choppy, and she's covered in as much dirt as I am today.

"Get her Black A!" a man yells on her side. Her trainer, no doubt.

She screams and runs at me, knocking me to the ground. My head slams on a rock as I fall. Stars dance behind my eyelids, pain drilling into my skull. I want to cry, but warriors don't cry, that's what Black Hat told me.

The girl slams her fist into my eye over and over, a flash of white light and pressure with every fist to my face as warm blood presses from my face. A piece of me wants her to win, she looks so hungry, but if I lose too many I will disappear like the others.

"Come on Brown 5!" Black Hat shouts. Using the last bit of strength I have, I reach for the rock behind my head and pull it from its purchase in the ground.

Opening my injured eye, Black A straddles my body with both hands fisted in the air ready to pummel me. Before she can lay another hit on me, I slam the rock into the side of her head, throwing her off me.

She falls to the dirt floor in a tangle of bony limbs. I rush over to her with the rock in my hand. I straddle her body and begin to beat her over and over with the small rock in my hand. The sound of skin ripping, bone cracking not bothering me at all. The cut on my thumb from that stupid rat, bleeding and stinging not slowing me down. All I can think about is food, the praise I'll get, and a maybe a warm bath.

Instantly a hand is cupped around my neck and it's like a numbness washes over me. Relaxing me. I'm lifted off the girl and onto my feet. The bloody rock falls from my aching fingers as I stare blankly ahead at nothing in particular out of my good eye. A haze of compliance surfing through me like I was injected with a drug they used to give me when I was defiant.

I lift my chin, blow out a steady breath and push it down deep hoping one day I'll forget this world.

Forget what I'm capable of.

Forget the savage acts I've done to survive.

Just like I forgot who I was before I became Brown 5.

ALESSANDRA

Present

Peeling back the warm foil enveloping the burrito, the smell of chicken, beans, and rice dance in a rhythm that has my stomach growling with mercy. My eyes nearly roll into the back of my head as I double fist it, and shove as much as I can into my mouth.

I don't take dinner breaks lightly, and I certainly don't take burrito breaks less than serious. The passenger cruiser door opens, and Raven slides into the seat with a bag from We Love Coneys.

Raven is my new partner. She has jet-black hair that is pulled into a tight ponytail. High cheekbones with a natural glow, and hard brown eyes. So naturally, she's beautiful. But with that flawless package comes her inexperience with the Las Vegas Police Department. She's a fucking rookie, and I got stuck with her.

Nobody wants the new guys. Why? Because they're a stickler for the rules, and still wanting to make the world a better place. That will end quickly the first time she has a homeless guy throw his shit at her, or when someone tries to stab, shoot, or spit on her. Her view on being a police officer will go from trying to make the peace, to just trying to make it through the fucking day.

"Anything on the MDT?" Raven asks, deep throating her foot-long hotdog. I raise a brow at her skill, before eyeing the terminal. The Mobile Data Terminal is a computer that relays messages from dispatch and other law enforcement in the area. I can look up anyone, and see who they are in a matter of a couple of clicks.

"There is a 413, and possible 420," I inform around a mouthful of food. My chocolate brown hair that escaped my bun gets in the way of my eating, and I blow it out of the way.

She looks at me with a puzzled look, conveying I might as well have been speaking in a foreign language.

"Person with a deadly weapon and a possible dead body," I tell her, not one-hundred percent sure that is even right. I have only been on the force for little over a year.

"That's right," she sighs, shaking her head.

"You'll get them, just takes time," I coax her. We used to just say what the hell was going on, but we moved to codes. Why, I don't know. To make our lives harder.

"I've never seen a dead body," she says softly, licking the cheese off her thumb.

I shrug. "You get used to it." I remember my first dead body. The smell, the stoic look on its face, and the color of the skin a hue of purple and black. A woman was held at gunpoint for her car and she fought the suspect off instead of just giving him the keys, granting her a bullet to the neck in front of the local food mart. It didn't faze me like I thought it would. I thought I'd be up all night with the look of the victim's face haunting me. I slept like I do every other night; hard. Besides, there's much worse things out there than dead bodies. Society just doesn't know it because we keep the monsters hidden from their everyday life. "What my co-deputies don't understand though, is the best way to catch a criminal, is to become one yourself. Walk amongst them, see things through their eyes, understand them. Then you can separate those who made a mistake from those that deserve to have your Taser up their ass."

She cuts me a look that would suggest I'm the Wicked Witch of the West and I just dropped a goddamn house on Dorothy.

"They're people, with lives and families, how can you say that?" she furrows her brows offended.

"Because you don't see anyone as people on the job anymore, you'll learn." I take the last bite of my burrito. "Or you won't."

A loud rumble races past me, and I jump in my seat. A rush of adrenaline tingling through my body as I lose my breath. Jerking my head to the left there's three motorcycles parking just ahead in a no-parking zone. The Sin City Outlaws to be exact.

Their bikes are shiny and full of chrome, their bodies clad in leather and tattoos. They're rugged and instill fear and sexual desire into citizens who come across them.

They never obey the law and why should they, everyone is in their pocket and if they aren't, they look the other way because of who they have in their pocket.

"Oh. My. God. Is that?" Raven sits up in her seat, looking through the windshield like a celebrity just flaunted their way across the street. The Sin City Outlaws are notorious for their ruthless way and reckless abandon for the law. They're as gorgeous as they are lethal. Their mug shots have been flashed along the TV and newspapers so much they are celebrities in their own way.

Did I mention my best friend in the whole wide world is knocked up by their president? Jillian, of all people, fell under the spell of Zeek, the King of Sin. I'm the friend with no morals and labeled as slutty, so how this happened to naïve little Jillian I have no idea. Maybe, I'm losing my charm I think.

"That one has a weapon," Raven points through the windshield. "And you're surprised?" I ask, tossing the wrinkled foil on the floorboard. It's illegal to carry in Vegas, but nobody messes with Sin City Outlaws MC. You fuck with them, it's the last time you'll be fucking anything. I stay clear of them, but my patience is wearing thin. Fast. The arrogant sons of bitches break laws right in front of me just because they can and it is starting to get under my skin.

Looking up, I spot the one that displays a nine-millimeter in a brown-leathered holster. He has long hair pulled into a bun. His shoulders and chest are so broad and built, the leather cut that displays his club's colors proudly can barely contain it all.

His eyes sweep across the street like he's stalking a prey. His stance wide, and arms crossed like he's looking for a fight.

He emits control, dominance, peril, and I would be lying if I said deep inside he scares the shit out of me just as much as he excites me. Berating thoughts of lust and annoyance swim in my head causing a tension headache to flare. Why can't they be fat old guys that can barely reach their handlebars? It would make it easier to avoid them if they weren't so good looking.

Two other men step up behind him, gathering his attention and I snap to my duties of law enforcement.

"The one that looks like Tarzan is Felix. He's the Vice President. The redhead with the menacing look on his face is Machete, and that David Beckham looking one is Mac. The one with the boyish good looks is Gatz," I tell her, my eyes sweeping across the sexy, savage crew. They're death in a gorgeous package, and they control Vegas - including me. Chief of police told me to let a senior officer handle them, meaning they're a dirty cop and The Sin City Outlaws will get away with whatever they want. I'm not stupid, I also can't do anything about it. Chief Lopez is a bitch on heels, and you don't want her up your ass.

"Oh, I know. We did a class just on the Sin City Outlaws. The president is missing though, where is Zeek?" she observes. Raising a brow, I suddenly notice he's not with his crew either. Good, he needs to be with his Jillian. She's carrying twins and is about to pop at any minute. "Is it true you're friends with the president?" Raven asks with eager eyes. My teeth clench and I shoot her a ridiculous look. Thanks to my best friend, I'm associated with the MC and I don't even converse with them. It's great. Not.

"No, I'm not fucking friends with any of them. They're the enemy, stay clear of them, Raven," I advise hatefully. "They'll eat you up and spit you out in the middle of the desert with the rest of the unmarked graves dug by the Outlaws."

Putting the car in drive, I carefully drive around the Sin City Outlaws. Felix's head slowly raises and his hooded eyes find mine. They're ominous and full of power and hostility. They pull me into the gates of hell with the warmth they emit, and it takes everything I have to look away. A knot forms in my stomach as I drive past him. Fighting the compulsion to look in the rearview mirror to catch one more glimpse of him.

"731, two suspects acting suspiciously near Frank 24. Gray shirt, gray pants, other suspect unclear." The dispatch crackles through the speaker.

I grab the radio and Raven looks at me with a confused look. I normally avoid vague calls, but Sin City Outlaws has me riled up and I need something to take my mind off things.

"731 copy, we'll take it. On our way."

"731 acknowledged."

Flipping the lights on, I push my boot onto the accelerator and go from fifty to seventy in seconds. It's not the newest vehicle on the force, but she still has some pep in her.

Pulling up to the residence, it's an old trailer with no underpinning underneath. A blue '87 Chevy sits on bricks with the tires torn off it and the front lawn is littered with trash and stray tools.

"Wow," Raven mutters under her breath. Getting a good look at my surroundings I take the shit pile in. It's not the worst I've seen, but I wouldn't expect a high piece of ass to waltz out of that double-wide trailer either.

"Just keep your guard up," I advise her.

"731 arrived at the scene 1400," I inform dispatch of our arrival and time. It's crucial we inform them of the time stamp because if we don't contact back within a certain amount of time, dispatch will do a status check to make sure we have a handle on the situation, if we do not reply, they send back-up immediately.

Stepping out of the cruiser I lock it, as I do every time. I don't need a crack head slipping in behind me and taking off with my fucking car. The Chief would have my head for that one.

The air is thick and smells of gasoline and sour trash. It makes my nose scrunch in distaste, as I look around for any suspects.

A short bald man steps out of the house, the screen door that's void of screen slamming against the doorframe.

"Well, look who it is, the fucking pigs!" he heckles around a cigarette hanging out of his mouth. He's wearing a greasy gray shirt, and gray torn sweatpants. His stained whitie tighties a sight to behold.

"Why don't you come down here, sir?" I suggest in a serious tone, wanting him where I have full control of the situation. First rule of being a cop, trust few.

"Did I do something wrong?" He tilts his head to the side, rubbing his junk like he has a farm of crabs living in there.

"Arrest that sum-bitch!" A woman flies out the front door, the screen-less door nearly slamming into her face as she points at the man. She's wearing a gown printed with little duckies wearing pink shower caps. It's two sizes too small, giving a full view of her pink panties that look to be period panties with the number of stains on them. *Be a police officer like your dad they said, it will be great they said.* How he did it for so long, I ask myself at least once a day.

"What's your name, ma'am?" Raven asks, her hand on her weapon. I notice her hand is shaking, she's scared and if I can see it, everyone can. We need to work on that, if the suspects notice, they'll play it against her. Like a dog, once it smells fear you're fucked.

"Oh, you don't know what you're talking about, Lucile!" The man shouts in the woman's face as he slowly makes his way down the steps.

"Hell I don't, Harold, you took my weed and you're going to

give it back!" She screams so loud her voice gives out, her face red like a cherry tomato. Not even caring she admitted to having a controlled substance or that we're even here from the looks of it.

The man laughs, finally reaching the bottom step. He places his hands on his hips towering over Lucile. "I ain't giving shit back," he says with a southern twang.

Lucile punches Harold on the bridge of the nose and he falls to his knees howling, while Lucile climbs on his back, slapping him recklessly.

"You dick-less momma's boy. I sucked creepy Stevie for that weed, and I'm gettin' it back!" she demands, riding Harold like a wild bull into the grass.

Shit. Quickly I pull out a pair of gloves and slip them over my hands. Who knows what creepy Stevie may have given Lucile after all. Stepping forward, I intervene and grab Lucile by the arms, and she begins to kick and buck in my hold. My knees ache as they press into the ground trying to keep control, and the smell coming from her makes me choke on the air entering my lungs.

"If you don't calm down I will hog tie your ass!" I threaten her, and she eases in my grasp.

I flip her around on her stomach with force and slam her into the dirt. I press my knee into her back and she cries out in pain as I fish her hands out from underneath her before handcuffing her. I'm not going to lie, this part excites me. Having the training I need to control people two sizes smaller or bigger. I'm the law, and I can put anyone down. It's a good feeling.

"What are you doing? He's the bad guy, he's the one smoking all my weed, man?" she laughs with a dopey tone, squirming beneath me like a fish out of water.

I glance over my shoulder to see if Raven has everything under control with Harold. She's struggling trying to cuff him, and he's finding it hilarious. *Damn it!*

Pushing myself up from a laughing Lucile, I step up behind Harold and lay my boot into the back of his leg. His knees bite into the desert floor and I kick him in the back until he falls face first into the ground. Raven nearly sits on his head as I grab his meaty hands and handcuff him as well.

"Sorry," she mutters, and I snap an angry glare at her verbally expelling her weakness in front of everyone. It would have been different if it were just her and I in the car, but saying it here in front of the suspects is not something you do.

"You have anything I need to know about?" I ask, searching the sides of Harold's body.

"Just a giant dick!" he cackles, and I roll my eyes at his ego.

"Really? Because, I'm not finding a*nything* that resembles that in the slightest, sir," I retort seriously, and his eyes furrow with surprise at my flippant etiquette. Most police officers don't say such things, but I'm not most cops. Not by a long shot, I know that and it both bothers me and drives me. My whole life I have been the third wheel in everything, and never knew why I felt that way.

Reaching into his pocket I find a dime size bag of weed and some ecstasy pills. I open it and smell the weed, it's strong and fresh. Creepy Stevie must be good at what he does.

My brows furrow remembering seeing a family asking for money at a corner this morning.

I'll sell this and run by there and give them the cash. I bet I can get a couple hundred out of this at least. I don't see it as being a dirty cop, more like Robin Hood. Kind of.

"That's mine!" Lucile wails, kicking her legs like a child having a tantrum.

"Not anymore," I mumble under my breath, shoving it in my pocket.

Raven's mouth pops open and I give her a look to shut it.

"731 status check?"

Grabbing the radio on my shoulder, I turn my head toward it.

"731 situation handled."

"Roger that."

My cell phone rings in my lower pants pocket, but I ignore it. It's my personal phone and it can wait.

Pushing off Harold I blow out a steady breath. "So, I can arrest you both for resisting arrest, domestic violence, and posession, or you can both kiss and make-up and take a fucking shower. What's it going to be?" I ask, fidgeting with the right glove strangling my wrist.

My phone begins to ring again, and Raven juts her chin at me to take it. "Uncuff them," I inform her, walking toward the cruiser.

Pulling the gloves off, I fish my phone out and finding two missed calls from Jillian.

Returning the call, I watch Raven get in Harold's ass for giving her a hard time. She can be a little bad ass if she wants, she just needs a little push.

"IT'S TIME!" Jillian pants into the phone and my spine races with goosebumps.

"Time?" I ask startled. It can't be. I'm across town!

"My water broke. IT's time," she sobs.

"Oh my God, I'm on my way!" Shoving my phone in my pocket I open the cruiser door.

"Come on Raven, we need to go. NOW!" I demand. She looks at me puzzled as she un-cuffs Lucile.

"Everything okay?" she asks, walking my way.

"Move your ass, woman!" I holler at her. Lucile and Harold stand next to each other staring at us like we've lost our minds.

I don't even wait for Raven to shut the door before I pull out of the driveway.

"What about my weed?!" Lucile hollers jogging after us.

"731 take me out of service."

"Copy that," dispatch replies.

"What the fuck are we doing?" Raven asks with fear laced in her voice as jet out of the vicinity.

"Jillian is having her babies, I have to be there," I tell her, flipping the lights on.

Raven looks at me with furrowed eyes. "Can you do that? Is this even okay to do while on the clock?"

"I don't really care," I sneer.

Feeling her eyes on me, I look her way finding her staring at me intently. Her dark eyes trying to size me up.

"What?" I finally ask.

"I swear this is like the movie *Training Day*, and I'm riding with Alonzo." She shakes her head looking out the window.

I smile and don't say anything because she won't agree with what I have to say. And that's Alonzo was a smart motherfucker when it came to running the streets.

Heading toward the hospital there's an accident with ambulances and a fire truck, the scanner is going haywire alerting everyone of a truck that caught fire so I have to go around, adding at least another fifteen minutes.

"So are you the godmother or something?" Raven asks, smoothing the wrinkles in her pants.

I eye her, curious why she'd ask that. "I don't think so. I don't know anything about kids, Jillian would be a fool to leave her kids to me," I snort.

"At least you have a best friend," Raven whispers, the dread in her tone making me look back at her. She glances at me and I see a darkness in her eyes that I've never seen before. The depths of her eyes show hurt, and a rough life. I give a tight-lipped smile.

"You got me," I offer, and she smirks and looks out her window.

"Yeah," she mumbles, as if I'm not good enough. I'm not hurt, I only offered it because I think we could kick it and be good friends, but there is something there that tells me she has a wall I can't get over.

Parking in front of the hospital, I turn the ignition off and take a long pull of my iced coffee that is now melted thanks to the desert heat.

A loud roar erupts from beside me and I jump so hard I spill my coffee down the front of my uniform, dropping the cup between my legs.

"Shit!" I squeal, quickly grabbing the spilling cup and up-righting it.

Growling, I look up finding Felix and his men parking right in front of me, an arrogant smirk pulling on his sharp face. That motherfucker!

Jerking the door to my cruiser, I get out. My arms outstretched coffee slips down my arms and drips off my fingertips. My hooded eyes slowly lift to Felix, my right brow raised.

"Do you get off on being an asshole?" I bite through clenched teeth. Anger poisoning my reason and common sense, I stomp toward him, my department issued boots slamming into the cracked sidewalk.

His brows furrow slightly as he tries his hardest not to smile at my temper.

Getting close, he towers over me, the smell of gasoline and cologne dancing around me in a hypnotic euphoria. My neck is cricked back to look at him fully. The gray in his green eyes reminds me of the color of steel concealing a criminal in prison. Cold and merciless, much like his personality.

"Jillian might have gone soft and got knocked up by one of you dipshits, but I'm not her. In fact, when the time comes, and it will, I'm not going to throw cuffs on you and take you in, no. I'm going to drive you out into the desert and beat you with my fucking nightstick!" My voice shakes with hostility.

"Sounds like my kind of Friday night," he smarts with a curled lip. "What time should I pick you up?" He comes on to me, and I blink rapidly. His dark but captivating eyes sink into me, clawing out feelings I've never felt before. Fear? Lust? I look away, not liking the way his stare makes me feel. His body looms over me, snaking my body heat away and replacing it with something cold and savage.

"Just stay out of my way," I warn. "That goes for your fucktard prospects too."

Felix's face hardens, and his eyes search his men wildly. Is he embarrassed? Or is he waiting to see if one of his men come at me for the disrespect I just spat at them.

"And here I thought Jillian was the queen of bitches, but I gotta say... you take the crown, Blue Bird." He mocks, his men laughing behind him. I don't find it funny, I don't find any of them funny. They're savages and killed Jillian's father. How she can overlook that is beyond me.

Losing control, I shove him, pushing him half a step back. He's hard beneath my hands, and my heart skips a beat at the contact.

"I swear to God I will tase you in the nuts!" I reach for my Taser, and he chuckles like I just made a joke. *Gah, I want to claw his fucking eyes out!*

"My best friend might have married one of you, but that doesn't make us friends—"

"Sure as fuck doesn't, that is one thing we can agree on!" he reiterates, his men agreeing by nodding.

"Good, then stay out of my fucking way," I point a sharp finger at him in warning.

He steps forward, his chest flush with mine. I suck in a tight breath, a weight on my chest making me feel like I'm about to combust at the seams. I'm scared of this man and what he's capable of, and here I am poking him with a fucking stick.

"Or what?" he snaps hastily, challenging me. I swallow hard, looking around nervously. His men stare at me intently. Their poses conveying they're ready to take me down with a snap of Felix's fingers. Raven is pale and looking at me like she might throw up from the altercation. Blinking from my stunned state I lift my chin and shoulders.

"I may not be able to arrest you because you're a dirty son of a bitch, but I'll make your life a living hell," I whisper, my eyes never leaving his. I'll pull him over just to pull him over. I bust a tail-light just so he has to pay for it to be fixed, and I will arrest every chick I see with him for solicitation.

"I'm the fucking king of hell, baby. If you haven't noticed," he says with a rugged voice. The darkness in the depth of his eyes telling me if anyone is going to hell, he'll be the one ruling it.

Maybe so, but I won't make it easy on him.

"Boys are so cute thinking a man runs hell," I sneer, propping my hand on my hip right next to my gun.

His nostrils flare as he silently looks into my eyes. The tension, hostility and something else lingers between us as thick as the Vegas heat.

"I hate to break this up, but Jillian is about to give birth and Zeek is going to kick our asses if we aren't there," Mac interrupts mine and Felix's staring contest.

Huffing, I take a step back and walk around him, Raven running up behind me.

The hospital smells like lemon and antiseptic. The fluorescent lights bright and ugly, and showing every bit of dirt and grime on the walls and broken tile.

Striding to the reception desk, a woman with short red curly hair types away at a keyboard.

Her gaze flicks to mine for a brief second before looking back at her screen.

"Can I help you?" she asks lazily.

"My friend was just rushed in having a baby, her name is Jilli—"

"Second floor, room three," she replies, eyes glued to the screen.

"Thanks," I raise a brow and head toward the elevator where all of the Sin City Outlaws piled in. The doors closing in on a shit-eating grin plastered across Felix's face.

"I really hate that prick," I grumble, taking the stairs instead.

"Really, because I thought you were going to kiss his face off outside," Raven huffs behind me.

My forehead wrinkles at her accusation. "I mean, he's sexy, any woman can see that, but I..." I swallow hard, trying to figure out what the hell happened out there. "But the law is the law." I give a curt nod, and might actually throw up at how cheesy that sounded.

Making it to the second floor, Zeek is talking to his men, and I take no time to push everyone out of the way to get to him.

"Where is she? Is she okay?" I ask frantically.

Zeek looks down at me with a hard stare, and I can't help but swallow hard. How Jillian got knocked up by him is a crazy thought. He looks anything but cuddly. His ink black hair has fallen in his eyes. His jaw hard and not a hint of happiness to be seen. He has to be packin' down there to make up for his asshole personality.

"She just delivered and is resting. You can go see her if you want," he informs with an unemotional tone. I flinch, as if I was asking to go see her. I was seeing her with or without his permission. She's my best friend. Practically my sister.

Entering the room, I find her lying in bed, her stomach not as big as the last time I saw her. Her dirty blond hair is everywhere, her face sweaty and flushed. She has a baby in each arm, and is looking down at them like they're her whole world. As if she's never seen or experienced a love like the two bundles in her arms have just gifted her.

"Hey," I whisper. Her head sweeps my way and her face lights up.

"You're here," she croaks trying to sit up.

"Don't, stay put," I insist walking to her bedside.

Smiling I pull the blue fabric to the side and see a Zeek look alike sleeping cozily.

"Oh my gosh, he's adorable," I coo. He's all pink and wrinkly looking.

She silently laughs. "They both look like their daddy."

"Did you guys decide on names?"

"Yeah. Meet Layken and Samuel," she looks back down at the twins. Her movements are slow and sluggish. I can tell she's exhausted.

"Very cute." I brush a finger over Layken's dark hair. She's just as beautiful and giving me baby fever like the fucking flu. I never knew what people meant by the smell of a baby, but being this close to Layken and Samuel I now know. It's clean, and sweet all at the same time. I could lift them to my chest and smell them all day.

"How are you feeling?" I whisper, looking her over. She looks a hot mess. Like she just went through war to be exact.

"It went really fast actually. I was having back pain all day, but didn't think anything of it carrying the twins. But before I knew it, my water broke and they were coming out!" she laughs, her eyes heavy and tired.

"Oh nice, you're like one of those moms who has their baby in the toilet because you thought you had a big lunch," I joke, and she nods as if she's agreeing.

"When my water broke, I thought I peed myself," she raises a brow at me and I cringe. "You should have seen Zeek's face when I told him it was time. I thought he was going to pass out."

"I'm never having kids," I insist. I'm tired just looking at what Jillian has gone through.

"You know, I'm not one to believe in love at first sight, but this... it's a testament that it really does exist," she tells me with a somber smile. Reaching forward, I grab her hand, and give it a squeeze.

"How are you? How was your day?" She shakes the tears from her eyes, inhaling a breath.

I scoff, before rolling my eyes. "Ran into the infamous Felix a few times. You know, how you deal with Zeek on a daily basis I'll never know, because I want to kill that Felix!" I grit every word, and Jillian just smiles in return.

"What?" I narrow my brows.

"Sounds a little familiar is all," she shrugs, rocking her babies.

My eyes flare with what she's getting at. "No! We are not

you and Zeek," I adamantly shake my head. I mean yeah, Felix is hot but he is so opposite of me. What could we possibly have in common besides wanting to kill one another.

Jillian yawns, before wincing. She needs rest, and I can't help but think she's trying to stay awake because I'm here.

"I'm on the clock, so I better go," I offer, but I really don't want to.

Jillian looks up at me with a thin smile. "Thanks for seeing us, I should be home soon," she thanks, slinking down in her blankets comfortably.

"I wouldn't miss it! Well, I did. But I was across town too," I admit, lifting my left shoulder.

"Go catch some bad guys," she whispers.

I laugh silently. "You have a whole crowd in the waiting room I could have a hayfield on," I tease and she just shakes her head before looking back down at two soft heartbeats that will forever change my best friend.

Stepping out of the room Raven is lost in a lust filled dazed with Machete. Frowning, I elbow her and she jumps to. God, I can't lose another one to a biker.

"Let's go," I tell her.

"How are the babies? Are they okay? Did she have twins? I heard it was twins?" she rambles behind me, trying to keep up. I hold my hand up stopping her firing of intrusive questions.

"They're good," I inform her. She nods, looking at the room Jillian and the babies are in.

I stride through the waiting room and my eyes catch sight of Felix in passing. He's sitting in a waiting chair looking bored, his elbows resting on his knees, his head bowed with hooded eyes following me across the room.

A cold chill licks up my spine, and my heart beats a little faster. Using my middle finger, I act like I'm pulling the top off a lipstick and apply my middle fingertip to my lips as if I'm painting them in my favor color. Flipping him off, as I look away.

I don't know what it is about that asshole, but I want to slam my nightstick in his gut and pull his gorgeous hair in a sea of ecstasy all at the same time. It confuses me and pisses me off. He makes me feel things I've never felt before. Dangerous, out of control, but oddly safer than I ever have before. He's a dangerous fantasy, and fairy tales don't exist in the city of Sin.

FELIX

"How's Momma doing?" I ask Zeek, rubbing my hands to-gether. He looks tense and stressed out.

"Jillian is fine, tough," Zeek tells me. He looks stupid with that blue gown on and cap. I should take a picture and post it to the wall at the clubhouse. "Did you settle the problem?" Zeek asks, concern heavy in his voice. Before Jillian's water broke we were knee deep in a conversation with the mafia. They want Sin City Outlaws as their muscle. I'm all for violence and striking fear into this city, but I reign my own control. My brotherhood condemns my punishments when I fuck up, not an outsider and surely not the fucking Mafia.

But they were clear. We submit, or war.

"No, the mafia is adamant. They want us to take over the Casino now that Frank and Cross are gone, and they want us to be their muscle. End of," I explain.

"Fuck!" Zeek barks, causing other families in the waiting room to scowl at us. Reminding us we are in a family environment and not our clubhouse.

"Look, I have this shit handled. Go be with your family, man." I suggest, not that him fucking knocking up a sheriff is my idea of a happy family. Not when you're an outlaw, but this is the path he is trying to pave for us and I have his back. Family and brotherhood, and I bleed brotherhood I just have to learn the family part. All I know. I trust my fellow brothers with my life, as they do mine.

"I'm trying, man, but you know as well as I, the mafia is not someone to fuck with and I don't want my club back in the throes of that chaos," he bites his bottom lip, his black hair falling in his eyes. He's right, no matter how I tried to tell him it's going to be okay… it's not. The mafia will fight back if we protest.

Zeek looks over his shoulder where Jillian and his newborn babies are held and back at me, a sullen look on his face. His forehead wrinkled with stress. I hate seeing him so vulnerable. I swear to God I'll never fall in love, look at this shit.

"Just, I want you to run the casino, Felix," he mutters, hesitation laced in the tone of his voice.

"You're kidding." I take a stand from the chair. I can't believe we're going down this road again, it was our dream to be out from under the mafia and running our own club. Doing our own bidding, and he's wanting to just give in? "We can fight this, brother," I implore him. I want to fight this. Blood, carnage, and war is what I know. Peace, that is a whole other fucking route.

"I know that, and we will. But right now I have to think about my family. Take over the casino, buy us some time to figure this out. Because when we tell them to fuck off… we'll be getting a war we may be able to win brother…"

ONE

ALESSANDRA

Two weeks later

Sitting in my car in my parents' driveway I strangle the steering wheel as I flick my eyes to the house. The one-story bungalow that has seen better days. Containing my step-mother, who I think is beginning to suffer from dementia. My father died on the job when I was fifteen, and nothing has been the same since.

Climbing out of my car with a long sigh I shut the car door with my hip and head up the steps and go inside. The door creaking and warning me it's about to fall off the hinges if I don't oil it.

The house is clouded with cigarette smoke, and the TV is blaring with the television show "Cops." Using my hand, I waft the smoke out of my face and fish the remote out from Dad's old recliner. Turning the TV off I look around for my deranged mother.

"Mom?"

"Oh thank goodness you're home." She pops her head around the corner, her hair pulled into an 80's ponytail on the side of her head. "I'm almost out of smokes," she coughs with a cigarette in her hand walking into the room. She has on a large Mickey Mouse sweater I've never seen before and skin tight rainbow pants. Where did she even find those?

I frown, my forehead wrinkling in confusion.

"Mom, you don't smoke," I shrug confused. I've never seen her smoke. Maybe she thinks she's back in the 80's. This is getting out of control.

Her eyes widen as she looks at the cigarette dangling from her fingertips, the wrong end of it lit. It's smoking like crazy and reeks of nothing I've smelled before. A small cough wracks her small frame as her lost eyes find mine.

Groaning I take the cigarette from her and rinse it in the sink before tossing it in the trash.

"Mom, have you eaten anything today?" I question, looking at the clean sink and counter. Yesterday she ate Manwich right out of the can, then she was up sick all night.

I think I'm going to have to get someone to come in and watch her during the time I can't be here. Maybe a live-in nurse or something. Dad's insurance should cover it. I just can't send her away to a nursing home. She's all the family I have left.

She throws a hand at me and makes her way to Dad's chair, flipping on the TV to resume her binge watching of "Cops." She sits there most of her days, lost in the show. Yelling how they do everything wrong because nobody can compare to my father. When my father died, so did she.

"I'll make us dinner," I mutter under my breath.

A dog yelps and I jump where I stand clutching my chest. A little ball of fluff sits on the floor looking up at me with a wet nose. A German Shepard to be exact.

"Mom, whose dog is this?" I ask, poking my head around the corner.

"Oh, there's a note on the table." She throws her hand at me as she gets lost in her show.

Eyeing the dog, I pick up the folded card.

Alessandra-

This is from the very same bloodline as Pete571, the same line that your father owned. I was on a waitlist to have him but I can't look at him and not think about how I failed your father as his partner. I wanted you to have him. He may not have been your real father, he did the right thing that day.

-K

Two emotions slam into my chest. Sadness and confusion. What does he mean he wasn't my dad? He's lying. He has to be. With my heart pounding in my chest like a sledgehammer, I barrel down the hallway to my parents' room on a mission to find some answers.

Entering their room, it's stuffy and dusty, the smell of musk strong as if the room hasn't had a waft of fresh air in years. The bed is perfectly made like usual, and a picture of my stepmom and father of their wedding day sits the bedside table. Passing the bed, I jerk open the closet door and a worn robe swings in my face, the slight smell of my stepmom's lotion swirling around me. Quickly I pull down the large box that sets atop of the closet, it has all of our family's important information in it. My dad always put our stuff in here since I can remember. Report cards, pictures, diplomas, all of it went in here. He wasn't much for filing things in the most efficient ways. Shuffling through the large amount of papers and folders, I pull out my worn birth certificate.

It doesn't show anything questionable or to suggest any red flags. The box falls from my grip and pictures from my parents' wedding fall freely to the thick tan carpet.

One of my grandma and dad smiling in a picture catching my attention amongst the mess. God, I miss them so much. My stomach knots as my eyes burn with emotion. Falling to the floor, tears pool in my eyes as I grab the picture, my fingerprints smudging across my dad's face. They both have blonde hair, and blue eyes. They look identical. I realize I look nothing like them with my dark hair, and dark eyes. My bottom lip trembles with the thought he may really not be my dad. Betrayal from my own family slicing through my chest almost too much to handle. The idea he lied to me becoming a reality, a sob wracks my whole body.

My dad told me my mother left when I was a baby searching to find herself, that she would be back one day. He told me she was a blonde bombshell that was too good for him, that he was lucky to have her in his life at all. I would always make a Mother's Day card for her, hoping one day she would come back. Hell, I still believed to this day she would.

Looking at the pictures of my dad's side stare back at me. Blonde, tall, pale smiles haunting me.

The proof is sitting right in front of me, yet I refuse to believe it. A sudden loneliness creeps up my spine, and bitterness fills my chest.

"Alessandra, you make your dad so proud, have I told you that?" Dad smiled down at me, wrinkles around his eyes as he sipped his coffee. The smell of his aftershave and coffee on his breath was soothing, and comforting in a way. It was my dad. I got an A on my spelling test and was nominated for the school's spelling competition and my dad is beaming with excitement, however, I could care less.

"Does that mean I can ride along with you this weekend?" I asked with hope. I loved riding in my dad's cop car watching all

the crazy people try and get past my father was entertaining.

"What about the spelling bee?" he chuckles.

"Nah, that's for sissies. You think I can shoot someone?" I asked with hopeful eyes, and my dad chuckled, pulling me into his side. I could care less about winning a medal or making it to the top of my class. I was different than other kids and I knew that. They always wanted to make their parents proud of their academics, and I always wanted to do something athletic or violent. I was a freak.

"Now how would I explain to the chief that my daughter is a better shot than me when you take down the perp?"

The dog whimpers, coming into the room, taking me out of the memory. He slides into my lap like were long lost friends. Tears slipping down my face, I clutch his chin and force him to look up at me. I remember my dad's dog very well, he was my best friend. They called him something stupid and I called him Rufus. Dad always told me to not treat him as a pet but as an officer, but it never stopped me from rubbing his belly and giving him the food I didn't want.

"They all lied," I sob, dropping the photo to the floor. Tears slip between my lips as I remember my dad's dog. I always felt like this was home, a place of safety and comfort but now it all feels wrong. Sniffling I stand, the note from Dad's partner crumpled in my sweaty palm as I stumble my way to my stepmom, the puppy following closely behind me.

Stepping in front of the TV, the card in my hand, I stare down at my stepmother. One I always saw as my mother as she has been there since I was able to ride a bike. Her and my dad were my parents, they cared for me and wanted me to succeed in life. There has to be an explanation other than my dad isn't really my dad.

"Was Dad really my dad?" I blurt with emotion, and her eyes pop to mine in a look of terror.

"What?"

"You heard me. What is this card about? Was Brock my real father?" I repeat with a louder tone.

"Why would you ask that?" she sneers as if I'm being ridiculous.

"Well, according to this note, either I'm adopted or I was stolen, so which is it?" I question, my eyes starting to sting. My heart aches at the memories of a man that may not even be my father.

She sighs heavily, sitting forward in Dad's worn-out chair. "Your father was going to tell you when the time was right he said. But he passed before that time, and I just couldn't do it. I already lost your dad and I was afraid I'd lose you too," she admits, tears filling her eyes to the rim.

My mouth drops, the sound escaping my mouth a cross between a cry and a scream. How could he not tell me the truth, we were so close? Not hearing it from him but hearing it from a weak ass note from a coward partner makes this ten times worse. It makes me question a lot of things now. Why had he hid that from me? What else is he hiding from me? They say my father was shot in the head by a drunk man who turned the gun on himself, but reading this card has me second guessing that too.

"When he died, did he really get shot by a suicidal suspect or was there more to that too?" Emotion thick in my voice. My dad was the best shot I'd ever seen, he bought me my first gun even. So some unstable man shooting my dad and killing him was something I've always thought was too unbelievable. He was a beast behind that badge and handled any criminal with ease, and a man who wasn't at peace with himself was the one to break my daddy? I don't think so.

"Mom! Answer me! Was Dad's death a cover-up?"

She begins to cry, her body wracking with emotion.

"I don't know, to be honest. I really don't," she whispers so quietly I almost didn't hear her. Slowly she raises her head, her cries softening and a look of confusion crossing her sun-kissed face.

"Have you seen my smokes?" she asks, looking around her. Her moment of clarity gone.

"You don't smoke," I mumble, biting my bottom lip in thought.

I wonder who my real parents are? I wonder if they are good people or bad? Why did they give me up? Actually, I don't want to know. My dad is Brock, and always will be.

He taught me to lead with my gut, and then follow my heart in everything I do.

My gut tells me there is something more to everything around me, and my heart is breaking at the thought of what it all means.

One lonely tear slips from the corner of my eye as I drop the card on the table. Hesitantly I look over my shoulder at the pup who is laying on the floor like a good boy.

My father was the K-9 unit for the department, and when he was killed his dog was too. His partner Kelly went nuts and quit, never to be seen again. Stress of the job, and my dad's death too much for him to handle. But now, I think more than what was let on lead to Kelly's breakdown and my father's death.

My dad helped those who needed help on the streets, and that often made him more dirty than he intended. There's more to how he died, and I think it was covered up. The only people that could possibly know that is the Sin City Outlaws.

Even if they killed him and covered it up, I need to know.

FELIX

Sitting at the poker table that has seen better days, I lay down my royal flush, and get groans from Machete and Mac, who slap down their shitty hands. Gatz chuckles as he nurses a beer beside me. His eyes smiling behind the rim of the beer bottle. He never plays against me because he knows I'll win.

Laughing, I stub my cigarette out in the ashtray and exhale a cloud of dancing smoke.

"Sir, we have a problem outside." Looking over my shoulder, I find our newest prospect, Bud, standing beside me, his arms behind his back like a fucking gentleman or some shit. His dark hair is slicked back, and his green shirt untucked from his torn jeans.

Pushing myself away from the table, Machete, Mac, and Gatz stand and follow.

Making our way through the casino, Bud explains to me how a couple of hang-arounds were giving some girls a hard time near the club across the street. It's Saturday night and the club is filled with biker enthusiasts and girls running around half naked in leather.

"It's always something," I mutter, pulling my gun from my holster.

Pushing through the double doors of the casino I find a man pulling a girl around by the hair, calling her a bitch. It unnerves me, and the grip on my gun tightens. I may have been raised by a bunch of criminals, but even I know to treat a woman with respect. At least a little.

"Do you know who I am?!" A familiar sassy voice echoes

through the building as she swings at the man.

"A fucking pig that arrested my brother-in-law!" Flame sneers, jerking the woman around by her brown hair. She elbows him, her other arm hooking around his neck in one swift move. It's not street fighting, it's trained. That's when it hits me.

It's Alessandra. Jillian's friend. The cop. She's got to be an idiot to come around here without Jillian in tow. Even with Zeek fucking a law enforcement, they're not wanted around here. Jillian is the only exception, and that is because Zeek is her damn armor.

Shoving my way through the crowd of muscle and leather, I nearly throw them on their ass to get to her. Last thing we need is someone seeing someone hassle a cop around our club.

"Let her go!" I shout, pushing Flame out of the way. He glares at me, his grip on her strong. His hard eyes flare with a silent challenge. Taking my gun, I shove it under his chin, accepting his challenge. "You have a fucking problem with my order?" I snarl, pressing the barrel into his neck. After a few long seconds, he reluctantly drops Alessandra to her knees and holds his hands up that are scarred. Rumor has it he was torturing a rival enemy with a blowtorch and it blew up in his hands.

Placing my gun back in its place I bend down to inspect her for injuries as she lifts herself onto her hands. Chocolate hair falls into her soft brown eyes. Her fingers dig into the gum-spotted concrete with rage. Her lip is split in the corner, and she appears out of breath. Slowly her angry eyes meet mine, clouding like the hostile clouds right before a dangerous storm. One that wipes out everyone and everything in its path without a morsel of mercy.

She spits blood and stands on her unsteady feet. I notice

she's out of uniform, wearing a white shirt tied at the hip and skintight jeans that hug her ass perfectly. I'm not surprised one of the men took notice of her. She looks like a fresh piece of ass.

Lifting her chin confidently, she cuts a menacing look at one man in particular, Flame. Like a gun went off at the Kentucky Derby she suddenly rushes at him like a wildcat. She's either really stupid, or that badge has her kidding herself.

Thinking fast I slide my arm out and hook it around her waist, hoisting her to the side and out of reach of Flame.

"Whoa, Blue Bird." My hands cup her silky arms as I try to contain her. She's so soft and creamy I can't help but wonder if she smells like honey or coconut. Taking the opportunity, I smell her nearness. Hints of coconut and spice matching her personality perfectly. She's a dangerous, beautiful package. My imagination paints the perfect fantasy of her lips wrapped tightly around my cock. A glare passes my face at the thought, not liking where my dick is going. She's a fucking pig after all. A rat that doesn't know loyalty if it slapped her in the face.

"I'm going to burn that pretty face, bitch!" Flame points at her, snapping me from mind fucking the enemy.

My head snaps in his direction. "Go. Now!" Warning in my tone. Flicking a cigarette at Alessandra him and the gathered crowd dissipate back to the club.

She tears from my grip roughly, and I can't help but want to choke the life out of her for being so goddamn stubborn.

"Why are you here?" I grunt.

"Are you fucking kidding me? That is what comes to your mind when one of your men attack me?" Alessandra shakes her head in disbelief.

"It's just a question," I growl. Testy bitch.

Throwing her hands out to the side she looks down, her

eyes clenched shut like she can't believe what she's about to say. She seems conflicted, lost.

"I don't know what the fuck I was thinking," her voice wavers with emotion. I don't like it. I've seen sluts cry, and club whores sob but watching Alessandra become emotional it unnerves me. "Maybe I thought I'd see if you had a party going." She shrugs, and I know she's fucking lying. No law enforcement comes around here unless they're in our pocket. They're terrified of us or scared to be around us because of our enemies. Blue Bird intrigues me, she's not like any woman I've ever known, nor law enforcement.

I can't stand cops, but more than anything, I won't tolerate a man that hits a woman.

Rubbing my chin, I look over my shoulder finding Flame within yelling distance.

"Did he hit you?" I question through clenched teeth.

"I can take care of myself," she rolls her eyes, rubbing her scratched up palms on her jeans. That sound in her voice gut checking me.

"From the looks of that lip, I'd second guess that, Blue Bird," I raise a brow at her bleeding lip and she flips me off. I want to strangle this bitch, but I need to make an example or I'm going to have members slapping women and that is not okay with me. I'm sure Zeek would fucking agree.

"Flame!" I summon him, and like the dog that he is - he appears. "Say you're sorry," I demand. His scarred brows narrow at me as if I'm joking. Tilting my head to the side I convey how serious I am.

"She fell. We were just helping her up," Flame suggests. He's lying, and I won't stand for it. Zeek wouldn't stand for the disrespect either.

Using my elbow, I slam it into Flame's gut making him

hunch over in a horrible groan. Fisting his stupid fucking Mohawk I drive my knee right into his skull. His eyes roll into the back of his head as he sways for balance.

Leaning over I get in his line of sight. "This woman is off limits, got it?" The words leaving my mouth confuse me. I hate her, she hates me. She's the fucking enemy and nothing more. Maybe I'm protecting her because of Jillian. Zeek would kill me if I upset his princess.

"Okay man, I didn't know," he groans. Flame shakes his head, trying to will the pain away. I shove him back on his ass. His fall slow and dramatic, like tipping a cow over on its side.

"Now you know," I mutter under my breath.

Standing straight, I find Alessandra looking at me with hard eyes. Her swollen mouth curved in anger.

"Why did you do that?" she asks ungratefully.

"Because I can," I answer matter of fact.

Flame is hauled off to the club to have our doctor tend to his injuries and I take a step closer to Alessandra. The alley walls secluding us from the public eye.

"So, you came here to what, let loose?" I ask suggestively, lust hanging from the tip of my tongue.

She looks up through hooded eyes, her hands fidgeting with the hem of her shirt.

Taking a small step, I invade her space. Using my finger, I tuck it firmly under her chin making her look me in the eyes. God, she's so fucking soft to touch, my hands itch to take advantage of her body and soul. That's what I do, I devour innocent women, and scar their souls to the point they're damaged goods.

"Were you going to fuck one of my men tonight, Alessandra?" I ask hastily.

Her throat bobs as she swallows, fire igniting her eyes as

she pulls away. She's a pistol and not the kind you love and shine every day with care. More like the kind you're scared to use because it may backfire on you at any minute.

"So what if I was? Why do you care?" She raises a challenging brow, her voice sharp. A burning sensation combusts in my chest thinking about her riding one of my guy's dicks.

"I forbid you to open your legs to any of my brothers, do you understand?" My rash decision comes from an unknown place. An insatiable hunger beading at the tip of my dick.

Her jaw drops, and her hands curl into fists.

"Who do you think you are to dictate who I screw?" she scowls.

My temples pound with annoyance and anger, done with this back and forth.

Leaning down my lips a hair's length away from her face, I intimidate her to the point she looks away and purses her lips.

"Maybe you didn't get the memo, Blue Bird, but now that Zeek is playing daddy... I run this fucking city. Therefore, I say who you fuck, and don't fuck."

Her chocolate eyes snap to mine, and I know I have her full attention. Which I want, I want her to look at me, to really see me. All of me.

They don't call me Felix the Cat for nothing. I will eat Blue Bird with a fucking smile on my face.

"We'll see about that," she sasses, turning her head so fast I swear I hear it snap.

"Next time I'm putting a bullet in your guy's ass if he so much as looks at me wrong," she threatens. Little does she know, I may put a bullet in her ass if she shows back up here without her bestie Jillian in tow.

Watching her climb into her black BMW, the tires squeal and she races off.

Fucking bitch.

The familiar sound of Zeek's motorcycle pulls up to the club and I walk over to him.

"So why are you here instead of home?" I ask, crossing my arms. Since Jillian spit out two kids, Zeek has changed. He's hardly here, and focused isn't even in his vocabulary.

Zeek's jaw clenches, as he rubs the back of his neck anxiously. Something is wrong.

"We got a problem."

Heading into the casino I follow Zeek, his shoulders are tense and the tick in jaw has me on edge.

"You going to tell me what's up?" I throw my hands out, tired of him acting fucking vague. He doesn't answer, just a jerk in his shoulder blade conveying he heard me but doesn't give two shits.

He steps into the elevator that our Uncle Frank used to go to his office at the top. I never go up there since we killed him and his henchmen Cross, went missing.

I always feel like Cross is watching, makes me paranoid.

The elevator doors ding and open and we head inside the familiar office. It's just like I remember. Big mahogany desk, lots of windows, a wet bar in the corner, and leather couches. I notice the chair is facing backward, and two men stand on each side of the desk. They look like twins with their hair buzzed and rifles in their hands. A pressed black suit fitting their built frames. Their faces long, and foreheads large.

Suddenly the chair turns, and a beefy man with splintering eyes pins me where I stand. A chill runs up my back stiffening my limbs. He has curly black hair. His face clean-shaven, and an unlit cigar sticking out of this mouth.

"'Bout time you show up," he snaps with an accent.

"Who the fuck is that?" I ask, my shoulders puffing out in defense. I've been handling everything here for two weeks and haven't seen anyone from the mafia till now.

"The fucking problem," Zeek informs.

The man chuckles before steepling his hands on top of the desk.

"You mudda fucka's kill the boss's main supplier and think what? They're just going to sit back and let it 'appen?" He shoots me a look that has me swallowing hard, my hand itching to grab my pistol. "I see ya kid, and these boys will pump lead into ya skulls. Got it?"

My chest rises with rage, my nostrils flaring by his tone. I flex my fingers ready to fucking do this. I'm blood thirsty and seeking violence like the night devours the light. Zeek gently grabs my forearm, silently asking me to stand down.

Exhaling a deep breath, I pull my hand away from my weapon and eye the man at the desk. Who is this asshole and why is he here acting like he's in charge?

"We killed one of their suppliers, and Cross is missing. You don't happen to know where he is, do you?" Zeek tilts his head to the side. After hearing that Cross was actually Zeek's dad and not the man that raised Zeek... I'm sure there are some unspoken words that need to be said between the two. The man sitting before us silently laughs, looking down at his desk. I can't tell if he knows of Cross's whereabouts or not.

"Sit," the man suggests with an unfriendly tone, ignoring Zeek's question.

"I'll stand," I grunt. The man bites at the cigar, his brows pinching together at my defiance.

"I'm Salvatore, and I'll be taking over the reins of Vegas. It's up to you boys whether or not you're a part of that endeavor."

"Pass," I clip, gaining a pissed off look from Zeek. He gets final decision on everything, or we take a club vote. But just looking at this snake I feel he's in the same snake hole as Cross and Frank.

Salvatore runs his hands down his face as if he's annoyed. Did he really think we would just roll over and let him take over?

"Why would we do that?" Zeek questions, coming off calmer than I obviously am.

"Someone needs to run Vegas—"

"We are! I thought that was the plan, one of my men would run this casino same as Frank did."

"Why in the hell would the bosses just hand it over to you cop fucking idiots? Do you know nothing about trust?" Salvatore holds his cigar out as if he holds the meaning of trust in his fingertips.

He's right, Zeek being with Jillian goes against not just club code, but the code of an outlaw.

"Tell me more about this endeavor," Zeek asks, taking a seat.

Salvatore grins like the Joker, thinking he has Zeek by the leather.

"I run this casino, and I run you and your men. You're my muscle in all dealings and transactions I might need," he explains, and with every word, I hear a hammer nailing our coffin shut.

"Why do you need us to be your muscle exactly?" I ask with a raised brow, and his eyes cut to mine.

"Because you know this city better than anyone," he responds dryly.

"My men are mine, simple as that," Zeek inputs.

"Wrong, they're mine and they will be at my disposal." Salvatore shakes his head, wiping his desk with a swipe of his hand. You can tell this man knows nothing about the bond of brotherhood, which is the foundation of every club. It's what Zeek and I are trying to achieve here, and if we accept this deal, we'll be back where we were when Frank was running shit. You won't know who has your back, and who is ready to stab you in the back to make it to the top.

"I've heard enough," Zeek informs, irritated.

Salvatore stands quickly, too quickly and I pull my gun out. It's my job to protect Zeek and I will kill this motherfucker and his guards whether or not I stand a chance.

"If you walk out those doors without agreeing to my terms your protection from the Mafia is deceased immediately," Salvatore threatens.

Zeek stomps to a stop, his head turning to the side.

"What the fuck do you mean protection?" I sneer, nobody is watching over our backs. We have our backs. Always have.

"You think everyone is just letting you run your drugs and guns, and looking the other way because of some biker trash intimidation? You think you knocking up a goddamn sheriff is just going to go unnoticed by your suppliers?" Salvatore chuckles.

"No, son, you fuckers are stamped with the motherfucking Italian mafia on your baby asses. You turn down our deal, you defend your own territory and answer for your transgression with crossing enemy lines." He points at us. I cut Zeek a concerned look, not aware we were being protected and by the look on his face, he didn't know either.

"Go fuck yourself. The Sin City Outlaws run this fucking city because we emit control and respect. You step on that and retaliation is the remedy for that transgression. Remember that," Zeek points at him. I smile. There is the cousin I know and love.

"You just signed your death certificate," Salvatore seethes.

"Don't threaten us with a good time." I wink before pointing the barrel of my gun at him. The two men standing guard instantly aim in my direction and my heart beats a little faster. My finger heavy on the trigger. A sly grin crosses Salvatore's face, but he doesn't order the kill shot. He's either surprised by the size of our balls, or we just asked for a fucking turf war.

TWO

FELIX

Pop! Pop! Pop! Pop!

Pictures crack and splinter before falling to the floor. Pillows are ripped, raining feathers and cotton, and the sound of females screaming and glass breaking echo through the clubhouse.

Instantly, I wake up.

Instinct kicks in and I roll over and fall off the bed to the grimy floor. I've been sleeping at the clubhouse since Zeek has been playing house. Crawling to the dresser in nothing but my boxer briefs I pull out my .45, making sure to keep low to the ground so I don't get slung with a stray bullet. I swing my bedroom door open and Machete comes running down the hall with an AR-15 in his hands, and no fucking pants. His limp dick and white ass in my line of sight first thing this morning.

Glancing down the hallway I can't tell where the gunfire is coming from, just bottles of booze exploding along the back wall of the bar. Nobody is in the club shooting at us that I can see.

It's a drive-by.

Standing up, I jog to a nearby broken window and point my gun out and start spraying and praying. Machete who has a death wish, kicks the front door open and starts firing off rounds hollering like a fucking gorilla.

Exhaust from motorcycles roar and speed off down the street.

"Did you see who it was?" I'm out of breath and not asking anyone in particular.

"MC, but I couldn't get a look at their cuts," Machete replies completely calm. He's not right in the head I swear.

Turning back around I notice the club is torn apart with bullet holes, and some half naked girls are crying. Dolly makes her way from the hallway, a black corset and booty shorts clinging to her tight frame. We call her Dolly because she looks like a doll with her black hair and baby doll eyes. She's a club slut and a good time if you're bored.

"What the fuck was that about?" she holds her hand on her hip, eyeing the club. She's not affected like some of the other girls, and it doesn't surprise me. Dolly used to be Zeek's main squeeze before he hooked up with Jillian. Dolly is used to carnage, you have to be to be with us as long as she has.

"Why don't you just go check on them?" I jut my head to the girls who are pissing themselves in the corner. Their makeup smearing down their face, and their hair looking like someone just smeared cum in it.

"Felix, are you okay?" Gia busts through the front doors, her brown and blonde colored hair wavy and down with a black bandana wrapped tightly around her forehead. Her leather jacket sexy as hell, and that sliver of stomach peeking above her ripped shorts tempting. She's not my girlfriend in any way but we hook up often. I also use her to my advantage. Meaning if I need a trade for my club, I send Gia to accompany them. I'm not an asshole, well, I am, but she knows our deal and is fine with it. Her and Dolly are the biggest instigators in this club, so not many women come near the main patch holders unless Dolly and Gia give them the okay. The only reason Dolly is still around after the shit she pulled with Jillian is because she was literally on her hands and knees begging Zeek to keep her around. This was her only family and had nowhere else to go. So we took a club vote and naturally, men like their dick sucked, so the votes swung in her favor. The only girl around here that has any pride is Tinker. She helps around the bar when she can. We got her a gig at a casino so she's been getting on her feet lately. We call her Tinker because she is identical to Tinker Bell.

"I love the smell of bullets and chaos in the morning," I mutter under my breath, tucking my pistol in the back of my briefs. Ignoring Gia.

"What the fuck was that?" Gatz asks walking out of one of the rooms with a concerned face and two .45's in his hands. Late to the show, as usual.

"Call Zeek, tell him our protection just ran out."

"Guess he wasn't bluffing then." Machete rubs his temple with the barrel of his gun.

"You got it," Gatz replies half asleep.

Inhaling the smell of gunpowder, I catch a naked Mac pouring whiskey into a half broken glass. His eyes closed as he guzzles it as if it were a glass of milk, his short hair a fucking mess.

"Am I the only one wearing fucking underwear?" I ask looking at my brothers.

Mac lazily opens an eye and grins.

"I had a good time last night," he winks at a couple the girls crying in the corner.

ALESSANDRA

"So you're telling me you have no idea who rained bullets into your club?" I ask Felix who is looking at me with a bored expression. He's obviously lying to me and wasting both of our time. I know I won't get anything out of him, but it's my job to try. With him not wearing a shirt and those low-rise jeans, it's taking everything I have to keep my eyes on my notebook and not his abs. He's a fine convict if I ever saw one.

"So who called the gun shots in?" he asks, crossing his arms. Ignoring my last question.

I roll my eyes, he knows I can't give him that information. If I did he'd probably race right over to the chapel across the street and shoot them in the head for tattle-telling and then I'd have the chief up my ass for breaking protocol.

Sighing I look past Felix at the club. It doesn't look like it did when I came here last night. It's a mess from the drive by. Bullet holes splintering into the building, glass glittering along the pavement, and bullet casings with spray paint around them everywhere.

You can smell the mayhem and uproar in the air, and I wish I were here to see it all go down.

"Can you just make this easy and tell me what you know?" I huff.

"Can you turn your badge into a fucking eight ball because that's the only way you're getting shit," he laughs, and I clench my notepad in my hand. If I was one of the deputies in his pocket I bet he would have given me something to report back to the station.

I wanted so badly to ask Felix for help last night, but I chickened out. The weight of everything just too much for one night. Plus, if I ask for something with nothing in return I will be in his debt, and that is the last place I want to be.

If he would give me something, anything. I could use it as leverage to get him to look into my father's case. I have to get in their dirty pockets to get that information though, but I need a fucking window of opportunity.

How do I proposition that though? Do I just come out and say, "Hey, let's be dirty together?"

"No, I don't know anything. Shouldn't someone with more experience be asking me questions?" he sneers, and that little hope of getting in his pocket fizzles.

I flip my notebook shut and sigh. I'm so sick of everyone seeing me as tits and ass, and not brains and a fucking loaded gun.

"I can interrogate just fine, it doesn't take someone with experience to –"

"You're just asking the wrong questions, Blue Bird," he interrupts.

My eyes shoot to his. He's got one arm tucked under his elbow while he lazily caresses the stubble on his cheeks. His hair is pulled into a messy ponytail and he has on no shirt. Tattoos of intricate ink claiming almost every inch. One, in particular, catches my eyes.

"I'd rather be carried by six, than judged by twelve."

He looks down noticing I'm staring at it. It's usually the other way around, I'd rather be judged by twelve than carried by six, but being an outlaw, I can see he'd rather be killed than a rat. It's powerful. I think I like it his way better.

"I like your tattoo," I mutter a little embarrassed I got caught staring at it. Sounds like something my dad would say in one of his wisdom speeches. My stomach knots thinking about how he isn't my father and I push the memories from my head.

"Are we done here?"

Clearing my throat, I nod. "Yeah, for now. I'm sure detectives and –"

"People better than you?" He tilts his head to the side and fire explodes in my chest.

"I really want to pistol whip in you in the side of the head." The words just come out of my mouth and his eyes flash with surprise.

"That doesn't seem very professional," he scolds, tilting his head to the side amused.

"You don't know anything about me," I retort dryly.

His hands fall, and he takes a step into my direction.

"Tell me why you were here the other night, I know it wasn't to *cut loose*," he implores his soulful eyes pinning me where I stand. They're cold and unfriendly, but inviting and offering protection at the same time. I have to look away, they see right through me and I hate the way they make me feel. Sexy, conflicted, aggressive. I feel fucking bipolar.

"Have a good day, Mr. Deluca," I nod, walking back to my cruiser.

FELIX

Zeek palms his face as he looks at the damage to the club. He stayed at his house with Jillian naturally with them just having the kids, so getting a call this morning we were hit has him in a sour mood.

"You mean to tell me nobody fucking saw a thing?" Zeek

questions harshly.

"We were fucking sleeping, man, by the time we realized what the hell was going on it was too late," I tell him, for the fifth fucking time. "Salvatore warned us, and he wasn't joking," I shake my head, my hands on my hips as I look the club over myself. I should have killed that asshole and sent our own message to the mafia.

"I'm putting Jillian and the kids in a safe-house," he mutters, his dark brows pinched.

"Good call, last thing we need is someone trying to get to them to get to you," I inform him. "Who knows how many clubs and gangs want us out of Vegas. We better sleep with both eyes open brother."

"If they touch my family, I'll burn this fucking city to the ground," he grits through clenched teeth.

"I'll be right behind you guns blazing, brother." I support him. I may not approve of him shacking up with the goddamn enemy, but I respect him and those kids are my blood. I'll do anything to protect them.

"What did the cops say?" Zeek gives me a look that pisses me off as if I would tell them anything.

"It was just Alessandra, I have her chasing her tail. I handled it," I smirk, and Zeek silently laughs. Alessandra is the typical fucking cop. Stupid questions, ya get stupid answers.

"All right, let's get this mess cleaned up and then I want every member in this club at church at six tonight. We are on lockdown, and need to discuss what the fuck that means," he says the last part lightly.

"Lockdown?" I ask puzzled. That's a first.

This is new for us, we've never had to worry about someone hurting us. We do the hurting.

ALESSANDRA

Having a short day at work, I decide to swing by Jillian's house. See the babies, and I'm curious if she has any details on what happened at the clubhouse.

Pulling up to Jillian's one-story house, I park in the driveway full of oil stains from Zeek's bike.

I hear a baby crying and the TV singing children show tunes. I go to open the door finding it locked. Furrowing my brows I knock, but Jillian can't hear me over the chaos.

"Jillian, open up it's me!" I pound against the door. Suddenly the door is ripped open.

"Hey sorry, Zeek called and ordered me to keep the doors locked. Come in," she says out of breath.

She has one baby in a sling around her and the other hovering over her other shoulder. One of her tits popped out and her hair is everywhere.

My eyes fall to the suitcase on the couch with clothes and bottles strewn everywhere. Is she leaving Zeek?

"You and Zeek calling it quits?" I point to the suitcase.

"Oh thank God, can you please take one?" she pleads ignoring my question, desperation deep in her voice.

Holding my arms out I take Samuel. His little face is beet red, and his arms are flailing everywhere.

"Why is he crying?" I ask, trying to rock him.

"I have no fucking idea. He's fed and changed, I think he's tired but he won't sleep! He never does and it's really starting to come between me and Zeek without having any sleep."

Pulling my phone out with one hand I Google how to get a baby to sleep.

Swaddling? I look the image over thinking I can do that, why not?

Tossing my phone on the couch I grab an elephant print blanket from the chair and set Samuel on top of it. Tucking his arms to the side I wrap the blanket around him tightly and sit in the chair with him. Rocking him.

His little eyes find mine, his crying hysterically quieting.

Jillian slowly walks into the room her face pale and mouth agape.

"How did you do that?" she asks in disbelief.

"Does he have a pacifier or a sucky thing?" I whisper, not knowing shit about kids.

She digs one out of her nursing bra and hands it over. I rub it on his mouth and he takes to it like I just offered him a sucker.

His eyes close, his little suckling the cutest.

Jillian plops down on the couch with Layken in one of her arms. I was going to tell her about what I found out about my dad, but right now doesn't seem like the right time. She looks stressed enough.

"Have babies they said, it'll be great they said," she nearly sobs. "I'm his mother and I didn't even think to look up how to get him to sleep. I've been calling the doctor nonstop and they've been telling me all these scary things and it was as simple as wrapping him up?" she throws her arm out at us, her eyes glossy.

"You have a lot on your plate, Jillian, you have mommy brain," I've heard that's a thing, not sure if it's true but my friend needs me to tell her anything at this point. "You are going to forget the most basic shit because your heart is so into this," I explain.

She sets Layken in a donut looking pillow thing and her head falls in her hands. She's overwhelmed.

"I'm trying. Zeek is trying, it's just..." she exhales.

I reach over and grab her hand.

"You can call me; I can take them off your hands for a few hours. Long enough for you to shower, sleep, maybe eat," I laugh, looking at the empty Pringle cans, and a package of crackers on the coffee table.

She laughs, wiping a tear from her cheek.

"Yeah well I'm being sent to a safe-house so that isn't going to be an option," she says with hesitation.

My eyes cut back to the suitcase, forgetting about it amidst the chaos.

"Safe-house?"

"Yeah, the club is in some shit and Zeek thinks it's safer if me and the kids are hidden. Can you believe this shit?" She shakes her head, standing. "*I* don't fucking run. Ever!" She throws a bottle in the diaper bag and looks over her shoulder at Samuel and me.

"I don't think I'm going to go," she mutters. "I mean, what example is Zeek setting if he's giving me special treatment? We are a part of his life now, and that means his club. I need them to accept me, and I'm not going to gain any of the members respect if he keeps treating me like a princess."

I sigh. "You're right. Everyone still sees you as the sheriff. You need to go by his way of life if you're going to commit to your relationship, babe."

Jillian holds her arms out, wanting her son back so I gently give him to her.

The sound of a car's engine can be heard running idle just outside. Jillian stands, looking out the blinds.

"Who is it?" I ask, looking down at Samuel's button nose.

I have no idea. They're just sitting there, Should I call Zeek?" she asks.

I open the front door to get a better look at who is parked

out front. A black SUV is parked in the middle of the street, and a man with a dark hat and black sunglasses stares back at me from the passenger side. His arm resting on the window jam casually. Cocking my gun, I take a step off the front porch and onto the grass.

"Can I help you?" I holler, walking in the direction of the SUV.

The sound of motorcycles thunders from just up the road, and the SUV squeals tires racing off. There's no license plate, so I can't run the plates.

Zeek, Felix, and Machete pull into the driveway and I instantly dive into protective mode.

"What the fuck have you gotten Jillian into!" I holler, replacing my gun in my holster.

Zeek frowns at my tone of voice, a look of confusion crossing his face. Felix whips the black bandana from his forehead and shoots me an annoyed glare.

Suddenly Jillian is racing out of the house in a fury of pissed off girlfriend and mother.

"I want you to explain right fucking now what is going on!" She shoves Zeek in the chest before he is able to get off his motorcycle completely. Nearly losing his balance, he looks down at her with a hard expression.

As they start arguing back and forth, Felix makes his way over to me.

"What happened?" he questions. I think about telling him to go find a more experienced cop but decide against being a brat. For now.

"Some SUV was just sitting outside with a man staring at the house. He didn't do anything, but he wasn't exactly asking for a cup of sugar either," I tell him, crossing my arms. The way the man's head was drawn, and looking at the house you could feel the intimidation behind him.

Felix bites his bottom lip, his chest rising with a large exhale. The way tension sets in his shoulders I can tell the club has stepped into a fucking mess.

"I'm not going to the safe-house, end of story!" Jillian shouts.

She pushes past Zeek and heads inside.

Zeek strides up to me, his forehead wrinkled. "You didn't see shit, got it?" he threatens.

I roll my eyes at his intimidation tactics.

"That's because I didn't see shit. Aren't you going to go chase him down and do whatever it is you guys do?" I point at the street as if the SUV will just reappear.

"You just don't know when to shut up do you?" Felix tilts his head to the side, eyeing me hungrily.

"It doesn't work that way I'm afraid." The softness in Zeek's voice takes me aback. He really does care for her. "Jillian wants Felix following you around," he informs.

"What?!?" Felix and I bark in unison.

Zeek smirks like the cat that ate the fucking canary, and I instantly want to rip his head off.

"You were seen with Jillian by a possible rival. You're at risk and Jillian thinks it's a good idea if you have a babysitter. So, baby, meet sitter." Zeek points between Felix and I.

"Jillian!" I roar, my eyes narrowed at the front door of the house.

She pops her hip out and crosses her arms. "It's happening. Get over it," she snaps before turning around and going inside.

"You're fucking kidding me! I'm not protecting a goddamn cop!" Felix protests.

"You are, end of. We will discuss the details after we get Jillian to the clubhouse," Zeek declares, walking past Felix and toward his house.

"You're taking her to the clubhouse?" Felix asks in disbelief. I'm shocked myself, she may be at risk here, but she'll definitely be at risk in there.

"She's my queen. My crew gets with that, or gets the fuck out," Zeek declares. "When I'm sitting in the chair behind the table, she is the one that stands behind me. Get that?" Shaking his head, Zeek stomps off.

Felix looks at me with a hard expression, obviously not pleased with the predicament.

"What? It's not like I'm entirely thrilled about this either," I huff.

FELIX

"When she's at work, she should be fine, but when she's off the clock I really want someone to watch over her," Jillian suggests. She's sitting on the couch with little baby rags folded on her lap. She looks every bit of a stay-at-home mother, but the flare behind her eyes tells me that spitfire sheriff is still very much there. She's not my friend, nor my family. We both know it but respect each other enough to appease Zeek. I'm just not used to being this close to a law enforcement without the need to run or defend myself. It takes a lot of trust to lie next to someone wearing a badge and I don't know Jillian enough to trust her. Biting my lip, I raise a brow at Zeek, not thrilled out of all the men around here he wants his Vice President; me, to play babysitter. I got shit to do.

Jillian looks at me with pleading eyes. "She's all I have left, Felix." I'm not going to lie, a piece of me wants her to get on her knees and fucking beg. That would very much please me to see a sheriff on her knees begging me for something. To see the tables, turn them and be at my mercy.

Taking a breath, I silently nod instead. Zeek killed her father, and though it wasn't entirely his fault it's still something he can't take back and will always be making up to her. Therefore all of us will.

"It will be taken care of, babe. Now let's get you outta here before we can't," Zeek demands with a cut throat tone.

Jillian gives a tight-lipped smile and finishes packing in the other room, leaving Zeek alone with me.

"I got her in this shit, I owe her this," Zeek explains, knowing I'm not happy about any of this. I don't want to roll over to the mafia either, but I'm starting to wonder what the fuck we got ourselves into.

"Why me, can't a prospect do this shit?" I ask. I hate law enforcement, probably more than anyone and here Zeek is fucking making me protect one. He'll regret this. I'll make this bitch dirty before the end of all this. Watch.

He points at me with a serious face, wrinkles forming around his eyes.

"Because you're the only man I trust enough to get the job done. Alessandra means something to Jillian, so you better stop seeing her as a cop, and start as a fucking kitten you're protecting from the big dogs. Got it?"

"Got it," I bite out. Little does he know, he's feeding her right to a fucking alpha dog - me.

"Look, you're my brother following me into this hell and you either have my back or you don't. But I need to know right now," he cuts the shit, and it hits me hard in my chest with reality.

"No, I have your back, it's just going to take me some time to wrap my head around why you would jeopardize everything we have, for her." I point in the other room, my voice low. We were raised not to trust them, and it's going to take me more time to reprogram my DNA.

He shakes his head, rubbing his cheeks.

"One day, you'll get it. Until then, you just gotta trust me."

I grab his hand and fist it firmly in a brotherly manner.

"I trust you. Always have," I say seriously. I've been by his side since I was a kid, and he's never let me down once. He's my cousin, but even more a brother. We have the same blood that runs deep for this club. There is no straying from that line of loyalty. My dad was killed by a rival gang when I was in my teens, and my mother was a club whore who ran out on us when I was an infant. I was raised by the club and would do anything for it.

"Then have my back, and protect Alessandra."

"I will. I do."

As attractive as Alessandra is, I want to put a bullet in that tight little ass. It's in my heart to hate her, to want to defy and wreck her. It's also in my nature to want to fuck the ever-loving shit out of her.

The question is how can I do both and keep my president happy?

ALESSANDRA

Sitting outside of the forensics laboratory I bite at my nails anxiously, the thought of what I'm about to do makes butterflies swarm in my stomach like a hurricane about to take over a major city. There will be no going back, the damage will be done and my badge will be scuffed with my defiance of the law.

Just as I think about turning around Billy walks outside with a black bag swung over his shoulder. His hair is more of an orange than red color, and his face is square and sprinkled with freckles. His cliché lab coat matches his geeky glasses perfectly. I watch him as he gets inside of his blue Mini Cooper and drives off.

I follow, as what I have to say to him I can't have cameras recording. At a stoplight I flash my lights at him and he glances in his rearview mirror at me. He drives forward pulling over on the side of the road. Not much traffic comes through this side of town, as it's the back way to avoid the highway. He must be on his way home; the other way would suggest he's going for groceries or dinner.

I pull in front of him and park. Getting out I meet him

between the cars and give a big friendly smile. The ground is hot beneath my boots, and the heat is so thick you can barely take a breath. There's cactus and bare desert around us, the city just beyond a giant broken chain-link fence not far from here.

"Hey!" I say with too much enthusiasm. *Shit, tone it down.* Last time we met, it didn't go too well. I'm surprised he even stopped, to be honest.

He gives me a nervous grin, the flare in his eyes telling me he hasn't forgotten either.

"Hey Alessandra, is there something you need? Did I forget something?" He looks over his shoulder back in the general direction of the lab. His tense posture telling me he's scared of me. The bulge in his slacks conveying he finds me attractive too.

I giggle flirtatiously and reach for the lapel of his blue polo.

"No silly, I just had a question." I wrinkle my nose in that cute little bimbo way I do. Using my looks to my advantage.

He looks down, his cheeks turning a shade of red. His Velcro tennis shoes kicking at the loose dirt.

"Oh yeah?" he mumbles through a too big of a grin.

"Hey, what evidence did you pull from those casings from the Sin City Outlaw's clubhouse?" I ask, trying to keep the lust in my voice so my personal emotion doesn't cloud that. Hopefully he buys it, I don't want to have to do what I did last time I needed information from him.

His head pops ups, his grin gone. My rose colored glasses turning a shade darker.

"You know I can't tell you that," he bites his lip looking out into the distance.

"Oh come on, I'm just curious." I twirl my hair, popping my hip out. Trying one last time to pull the information I need from him before having to do it the hard way. The risky way.

His eyes rake me up and down the words I want to hear right on the tip of his tongue.

"I can't... I'm sorry."

"Fuck!" I roll my eyes, my fingers straining like I want to strangle the fuck out of his geeky ass. My flirt innocent act drops like a sack of ice, and anger replacing it. His face drops as I suddenly whip out my Taser and strike him right behind the shoulder. The device vibrates my palm as it shoots an electric current through his small frame. His body spazzes and he falls forward like a dead weight. I look around making sure nobody saw, but it's deserted. I'm so going to hell.

"Why did you have to take the hard way," I mumble, unlocking my trunk angrily. Tucking my arms under his armpits, I shuffle him up and toss the top of his torso into the trunk.

"Jesus you're heavier than last time," I heave, tugging his bottom half into the small space. I begin to sweat, my heart beating harder at the thought of me getting caught shoving a body in my car.

Closing the trunk, it hits his head making him come too.

"Alessandra!" He bangs around, his voice in complete panic.

"Are you going to tell me?" I ask, leaning against my car. My arms crossed casually as I watch the dirt dance in the wind. My back is covered in sweat and tickles as it drips down my skin. Damn it's hot out here.

"Damn it, I can't believe you're doing this again," he mumbles to himself, and I silently giggle. Being a good cop isn't just about following the law and the rules you swore by. It's about knowing when not to follow and abide by them. I don't bleed blue, I'm a darker breed than the badge on my uniform will ever understand. If I can get a lead on those shell casings,

I'll have something to put into the pockets of Sin City Outlaws and gain their trust. I've gone too many years turning my head from my father's death. Not anymore.

My personal phone rings, grabbing my attention from the screaming man in my trunk.

It's Jillian.

"Hey, is everything okay?" I ask.

"Yeah, I just got to the club. I'm so out of my league here. I don't know what Zeek brought me to, but I'm not thrilled with this. I mean, I want to protect my kids, but the sheriff in me wants to run at these assholes," she huffs into the phone in one long breath. "The girls won't even look in my direction so he must have said something to them," she continues, with a hint of pride in her voice.

"Has he duct taped you to a chair yet, keeping you hostage from doing a sweep through for drugs and illegal guns," I laugh because Jillian would so do that.

She giggles. "Not yet, but he did threaten to tie me to the bed."

"Let me out of here, goddamn it!" Hollers from my car with a series of pounds against the trunk. I hold my hand over the receiver and step away.

"What was that?" Jillian asks with a concerned tone.

"I um, I have someone in custody," I lie. Jillian is my best friend, but she'd never understand the way I do things. Jillian is strictly rulebook, and I make my own rules. I fear it will come between us.

"Oh, I'll let you go. Just wanted to let you know we are here and safe."

"Good to hear. Thanks by the way for having me tailed!" I spit angrily.

"Anything for my friend," she replies sarcastically. Scoffing,

I hang the phone up and growl under my breath at Billy and his loud mouth. Hopefully Jillian bought that he was a suspect in custody.

Popping the trunk, he throws himself over the side dramatically huffing for air.

"It's not that bad, you're being a baby," I silently laugh, crossing my arms.

"It is when you're claustrophobic!" he blubbers. He's all sweaty, with his face beet red and nose running.

"You ready to tell me what I want?" I tap my foot in a bored manner.

He raises his head, his forehead wrinkled.

"It's got to take one crazy motherfucker to love you, you know that?" He tilts his head to the side. I can't help the smirk that breaks through my annoyed look. I haven't found my prince in shining tattoos yet, but I will one day. He will accept the good and the bad parts of me, and love me like a madman. One I should probably take into custody, but would much rather ravage me in the back of my cruiser.

"The case was taken from me, Alessandra," Billy's voice breaks me from my mental fairy tale.

"The main forensic, JT, took it and closed the file. Told me it was out of my pay grade. I overheard him telling someone else that nothing but a turf war would come of the findings. So I'm guessing that is why they closed it." He shrugs, and I drop my head defeated. I kidnapped a man and put him in my trunk for nothing.

"*But,* I did manage to get a name off a partial print on one of the casings before the case was taken from me, but I wasn't able to run it fully," Billy continues as he climbs out of the trunk.

This piques my curiosity.

He points at me with a sharp finger, his sweaty brows sliced inward. "If I tell you, no more fucking trunk. GOT IT?" he demands. Rolling my eyes, I put my hands on my hips. I can find other ways to get what I need out of him in the future so why not agree.

"Fine," I mumble.

"Apollo Bates," he heaves, wiping his forehead with his lab coat.

"Apollo Bates?" I whisper, not familiar with the name. Then again most of the gang members around here don't go by their legal name. They have nicknames. I'll have to run it in our database and see if it notes what gang he's with. Either way, it's something to bring to the Sin City Outlaws.

"Are we done?" he snaps.

Coming back to the conversation, I nod. "Yeah, thanks." He shakes his head walking past me. Reaching out I grab his arm to stop him.

"No really, this is doing something personal for me. I really appreciate it." My soft tone wipes his pissed off look away.

"I hope you get what you're looking for, Alessandra."

Letting him go I watch him get in his car and drive away. He really would be a great guy to hook up with… if I was into soft geeks. I'm not though. I like the bad boys, the kind that I can frisk for breaking the law, and have my way with right before I put them in jail. The kind that would have my dad turning over in his grave if he ever saw them approach his daughter.

ALESSANDRA

Stepping up to the Outlaws' club, I take a deep breath. The pistol in the back of my jeans reminding me that no motherfucker is going to be putting me in my place today. I was an idiot not to bring it with me before. Jillian is here now though, and if things go south, she'll have my back.

A man that looks like prospect due to his patch-less cut, holds his hand out, stopping me from entering the club and I shoot him an annoyed look. His head is completely covered with a red bandana, his square jaw sexy with its dark stubble, the side of it scarred. He has quotes of famous killers from all over the country on his arms and up his neck. Ted Bundy's words about Murderers standing out to me more than the others. Swallowing the dry lump in my throat, I clear my voice.

"Can you tell whomever it concerns that Alessandra is here?"

The man scoffs, his ice blue eyes cutting me where I stand. My hand twitches to grab my gun out of pure fear, but I resist.

"We're on lockdown, nobody enters without the say-so of a patch holder," he informs me dryly. My eyes fall on his name at this point, curious who he is. I've never seen him before. The Outlaws must be recruiting new members.

Bomber Jack.

I wonder what he did to earn that nickname. Actually, I don't want to know.

"Well, *Bomber Jack*, tell your president I have something he wants regarding this morning's shooting," I tell him with a click of my tongue. The man turns his head to the side, unsure of what to do. He was clearly ordered to tell everyone to fuck off, but what if he turns me away and the president wants the info I have?

"Don't fucking move," he sneers, the tone of his voice gluing my black boots to the asphalt. The man slips inside, and seconds go by. A chill races up my spine as I sit in front of the most dangerous club in the city, maybe the world. My heart is beating so hard it's making me anxious. I might actually vomit.

The man steps back outside and silently juts his head toward the door. Indicating I can enter the den of outlaws.

Stepping inside, the smoke is thick and heavy. "Porn Star Dancing" by My Darkest Days plays loudly. The lighting is dim, only a bright red light above the bar flashing on two girls making out with each other. A man that looks like the member Mac is getting blown by a skinny woman with pink colored hair, she's butt naked with a snake tattoo claiming her whole right side. I've seen a lot of crap in my wild days, but I feel out of my league in every way. *Where are Jillian and the kids?*

Pushing through the thick crowd, I seek out Felix or Zeek. The crowd slowly splits and my eyes fall onto Felix. He's sitting in a chair in the middle of the room owning it as if it's his throne. A blunt hangs out of his mouth, with smoke dancing around him like an exotic gypsy. He emits power and control by just the size of him and the look on his face. He owns the room without even having to move or say anything. His long hair is down and sitting on his strong shoulders. A black worn shirt pulls at his chest tightly and my fingernails dig into my palm with the urge to scratch him like a wildcat. To feel those hard abs beneath my fingernails.

Sitting on his knee is a chrome .45; his hand resting on the handle of it. His head is lowered, his gray eyes surveying the room cutting through everyone like a sword before finally meeting mine. I inhale a breath so deep my lungs burn from the smoke, my toes curl in my shoes and I have to remind myself to exhale.

Taking a step forward, two girls step in my way. One I recognize as Dolly, she used to give Jillian crap a lot, I'm surprised she's still around. The other woman I've never seen before.

"You lost, sweetheart?" The new girl asks. She's sexy. Hair pulled into a red bandana that matches her red bra pushing out of her black leather jacket. Her makeup is thick and very heavy, I bet if I licked my thumb and wiped it along her cheek I would see every flaw this shallow girl has.

"No, I know exactly where I am, thanks," I sneer, making sure she can hear me above the music.

"Excuse me, bitch?" Dolly tilts her head to the side. "You don't mouth to Gia and get away with it," she laughs.

"Move," I raise a brow, daring them to try and play with me. Gia reaches out in a striking manner and I grab her wrist and spin it behind her back as if I was arresting her.

She screams, and Dolly starts pulling my hair with her fake ass nails. Using my free elbow, I crack her in the face, making her fall to the ground.

Leaning in, I nip at Gia's ear. "I'm one bitch you won't be playing with, babe. Stay out of my way, or I'll shove my gun so far up your ass you'll moan my name. Got it?"

She doesn't respond, she just squeals, trying to stomp my foot with her skanky heel.

The music stops, and the crowd is pushed apart. Looking above Gia, I come face to face with Felix. His cold eyes looking almost amused at the altercation taking place. Crossing his arms, his head tilts back, his jaw ticking as he takes in the sight before him.

"Let her go," he demands, the sound of his voice raspy. Shoving Gia's arm one more time for good measure I let her go.

She stumbles, tears in her eyes as she looks at me with a look that could kill.

"Did you see that? Did you see what she just did?" she whines to Felix.

"Isn't she a cop?" A voice from the crowd states, getting

everyone riled up.

"Why are you here?" Felix asks.

"I have some information you want," I inform him. He scoffs, looking around the room like I'm insignificant. My heart pounds a little harder, the urge to go ape shit on everyone strong.

"It involves this morning's shooting, but obviously you don't care. So I'll just wait for the president of the club," I sass, turning where I stand. Before I make a step forward, I'm whipped around, a tight grip snakes around my throat and I'm slammed against the wall. Felix's cold eyes slice through me, his body heat radiating off of him. The feel of his fingers wrapped around my throat with such ease but exuding power, I can't help my nipples budding.

"Everyone get the fuck out!" he barks, and they obey immediately. Disappearing left and right.

Felix doesn't take his eyes off of me though, his clutch on my throat tightening. I swallow, trying to keep my composure, keep my heart rate under control.

"Spill it," he commands.

"First, I need something from you." The words are hard to get out. A maniacal laugh spills from his mouth, his grip slightly letting up. Leaning forward his lips brush against my ear and my knees buckle from the contact.

"I think my blue bird is a dirty bird," he whispers, and my eyes flutter with lust. "Am I right? You want in our pocket don't you?" He looks me deep in the eyes. I've done a lot of shady shit in my career, but right now I'm signing my soul over to the devil knowing I may not get it back.

"Y-yes," I mutter, my eyes stinging with the urge to cry. Feeling me cross the line of good to enemy.

"What do you want?" he asks with a softer tone.

"My father was killed on the job years ago, I think there is more to his case and I want to know what really happened."

"What makes you think I can find that out?" He lets go of my neck, eyeing me from the side.

"I don't, but I figured it was worth a try," I shrug.

"Tell me what you have for me in return and I'll think about it." He runs his hands through his hair and I sigh unintentionally. His eyes cut to mine, he heard it.

Looking down, I finger my bottom lip anxiously.

"There was a partial print on the shell casing from this morning. Apollo Bates, he's with—"

"The Lost Bastards, I know," he interrupts. "How did you get that information?" he asks with a tone of surprise.

Pursing my lips, I raise a brow.

"I can't go telling my secrets, otherwise why would you need me?"

His eyes rake along my body unforgivingly, and my brows narrow in on him. "You should have kept your legs closed, because there are no guarantees you'll get anything in return," he insults, insinuating I slept with someone to get the information.

My mouth drops. "I didn't fuck anyone!"

He scoffs. "I'm sure you didn't." His tone unbelieving.

He snaps his fingers and Machete steps from the darkness.

"Put her in one of the rooms," Felix demands.

"What?" I ask with a tone of panic.

Felix looks over his shoulder. "I'm ordered to babysit your ass when you're off duty, and considering you're out of uniform I'm guessing you're not working?"

"So what? You're just going to lock me in a room?" I ask in disbelief.

He shrugs with an arrogant smirk. "Yeah, pretty much."

Machete reaches for my arm and out of instinct I pull my gun from my waist and aim it at him.

"Don't fucking move!" I threaten. He stops, looking over his shoulder at Felix for direction on his next move.

"Jesus Christ, you must have a death wish," Felix growls. He stomps toward me and I swing my aim at him. My back begins to sweat, my breathing becoming heavier. *Where the fuck is Jillian?*

His eyes flash with an unknown look, his mouth pulling at the corner.

"You *are* a dirty bird," he rasps, and my finger brushes the trigger.

"Tell me we have a deal and let me walk out of here and nobody has to get hurt," I state with an unknown confidence. My hand aches to tremble, my heart slamming in my chest like a racehorse.

They both laugh, and Felix whips out with lightning fast reflexes and grabs my gun from my hands. My finger pulls the trigger at the last second, and a bullet lodges into the floor right next to Machete's foot.

"Jesus Christ!" Machete jumps back, and Felix glares at me. That look of humor gone now that he knows I would shoot him.

"What the fuck is going on in here?" A familiar voice echoes through the room. Looking over Felix's shoulder Zeek stands tall and shirtless. His jeans slung low on his hips, and stance wide.

His eyes fall on me and his right bicep ticks.

"Oh good, you're here." He sounds unamused.

"Not for long. I came and said what I needed to say, and now I'm leaving." I lift my chin, my voice steady and strong.

Zeek shakes his head, rubbing his chin as he looks around.

People stand in the corners, and outside their rooms as they watch the altercation.

"If you're here it's because you mean something to the Sin City Outlaws and I want to keep you safe as we get our shit figured out. I don't expect things to go south but I won't have anyone hurt on my watch. Everyone that is in this club is your friend and family no matter if they are a dirty cop, or from a different club. You treat everyone with respect or you answer to me. You have a problem with that, get the fuck out while you have the chance!" I sneer at his dirty cop comment. People from around the club eye, and nod in agreement.

But me, I start toward the door.

"You don't have a choice sadly." Zeek pins me where I stand. "You were seen with Jillian, so you'll be a target. I don't need someone trying to gain leverage over me because of you. Therefore, you'll be staying here when you're not working. You best make arrangements," Zeek demands.

My mouth pops open to protest, but before I can get a word in edgewise, Felix grabs ahold of me and throws me over his shoulder.

"What are you doing?" I yell, slapping his hard back over and over. Trying to kick him the balls, anything to defend myself. I might as well be hitting a wall because it does nothing to stop Felix.

He marches me down a hallway, kicks a door open and steps into a pitch-dark room. The smell of gym socks, and dirty crotch strong. He flips the light on and a disheveled bed comes into view just before he tosses me on it.

"Where are we?" I ask nervously.

"Stay in here," he points at me. I stand, anger pounding in my temples.

"I can't stay here. I need to go home, my mother needs me!"

I grit through clenched teeth.

"Your mom will be taken care of. I have orders to keep you safe, and that's what I'm doing." He slams the door shut, and I sit there shocked.

Does he really expect me to just sit here? Getting up I go and open the door, and Machete is standing there with his arms crossed looking at me with a murderous stare.

"Don't make this hard, babe," Machete begs. His hand slowly falling to his gun on his hip.

Growling with frustration, I turn around and slam the door shut. Remembering I have my phone I dig in my pocket and call my neighbor. Someone has to keep an eye on my stepmom.

"Hello?"

"Hey June, I'm out for… work," I lie on my toes. "Do you think you can keep an eye on my mother?"

"Sure thing, I'll bring some cards over," she informs sweetly.

Before I thank her, the door is slammed open and the phone is jerked from my grip by Felix.

"What are you doing?" I scream, standing ready to beat his ass.

"What do you not get about we are on lockdown, and your ass *is mine* for the time being?"

My face stoic, I can't help my panties dampening from him claiming me like a madman.

His head tilts to the side, a look of desire crossing his face. My cheeks burn with embarrassment as I look away.

He tucks a finger under my chin, making me look him in the eye. His body so close I can't help but rest my hands on his chest. It's so warm, so hard. My nails dig into his shirt, my pussy clenching with need.

"I know that look," he states huskily. "I think dirty cop wants me, don't you?" he asks arrogantly. Quickly I snap my hands from his chest, and try and take a step back but my legs hit the bed.

"Is that it? Do you want to straddle my lap while I pump my dick into that little pussy?"

My head whips up, my breath gone. My words stolen by this man with no regard for the law or manners for that matter. His harsh words sweeping in-between my lips and stealing my breath away like the outlaw that he is.

He leans in and a soft moan spills from my lips desperately wanting him to take me on this bed.

"Too bad I don't fuck cops," he jeers, taking me from my lust filled state. I shove him, needing him away from me so I can think clearly.

"Get the fuck away from me," I seethe. Angry with myself, pissed that I am getting lost in the broken beauty of this man. I've let my guard down and now look where I am.

"What is going on in here?" The familiar voice of Jillian echoes down the hall. She steps into the room wearing a black robe, her hair wet and eyes wide. She cuts Felix a look that speaks volumes.

"He's locking me in here!" I inform her.

"I asked you to look after her, not keep her prisoner!"

"Oh, I'm sorry, I must have missed that in the handbook of protecting a fucking cop!" he smarts.

Rolling her eyes, she pushes Felix out of the room and slams the door shut.

"I can't stay here Jillian. I have a job, I have my mother, a dog for Christ's sake!" I feel the urge to cry but resist.

She grabs my hand and gives it a tight squeeze. "I will make sure they are *all* taken care of, Zeek will. I just, I need you to try and let them do what they need to do. Trust me, you don't know what lays in the underbelly of Vegas, and from what I've overheard Zeek and the men saying... we are the target for every criminal in the three-state area. They're refusing the mafia's protection I think."

My eyes widen with this news, but with Zeek's Uncle Frank dead, and his right-hand man, Cross disappearing without a trace, it doesn't surprise me. Every club and gang around will want to take the Outlaws out and take their turf.

Looking at Jillian I want to slap her for putting me in this mess, but at the same time, she really is trying to keep me safe.

Guilt flares in my chest that I am crossing the enemy line and I have to look away from Jillian. I swallow that shit down and lift my chin confidently. Nothing is getting in my way of me and my family, especially my fucking conscious. I need to know what happened to my dad, and I will.

"I'll try and play nice," I whisper. And by 'try' I mean I'll try and not shoot Felix in the dick.

FELIX

I rub at my chin, eyeing the door that contains a fucking cop in my club. I cannot believe Zeek put me on this shit. Zeek is obviously trying to put our club on a different path than what his old man had us on, and I'm trying to see it. I'm trying to trust him and know that our brotherhood can withstand the repercussions that may fall in its wake getting to that path Zeek is looking for. But even with me having Zeek's back, keeping Alessandra safe is going to be nearly impossible around here. Jillian might be safe from people trying to kill her, but that's because she is Zeek's ol' lady. Alessandra isn't owned by anyone. She's fair game and is playing with wolves being here unclaimed. Zeek's order to leave her alone, be damned.

I'm completely shocked she wants in our pocket. The balls on her are bigger than some of our own members and that draws me to her. She's not weak, and the outlaw in me wants to make her weak. I want to break her, make her mine.

Growling I slam my hand into the wall, making Machete eye me warily.

I'm fucking losing my mind.

Jillian steps out of the room pulling her robe tighter, her eyes glaring at me like I'm the asshole.

"She tried to shoot me," I inform her, and Jillian rolls her eyes.

"She's a handful, but you have two hands. You'll live... maybe." She winks, before entering her and Zeek's room.

"Bitch," I mutter, flexing my fists.

Zeek strides out of the room with a beer in his hand and glances at Alessandra's door.

"So I know you didn't bring her here, why'd she show up?" he asks.

"She's a dirty little bird," I smile wolfishly, and Zeek raises his brows in curiosity. "Call the boys, it's time to retaliate," I pull my bandana from my back pocket and wrap it around my forehead. Needing to take this aggression out on someone for I fear if I don't, a pretty little deputy is going to be taking the wrath of this outlaw.

ALESSANDRA

Sitting back on the bed I glance around the room. It's not

clean and is basic. Bed, dresser, chair, pornographic posters. Glancing at the door I think about sneaking out, about going home to my comfortable bed, but I don't. Something deep inside me tells me to actually listen to what I'm told for once. Sighing deeply, I nose around the room. Opening the old dresser drawer, I find folded shirts, jeans, and spare bullets. I close it, and head into the adjacent bathroom.

It smells of grease and aftershave.

Running my hand over the fake marble counter I reach for the toothbrush. Eyeing it, I wonder if it's Felix's. If I knew it was, I'd scrub the toilet with it, but because I don't, I put it back in its place.

Feeling exhausted I go back into the room and open the closet, finding a bunch of shirts with the club's logo on it. I grab one and let the hanger drop to the floor.

I pull my shirt off, and then my bra before sliding the worn fabric over my head. That's when I notice the sleeves have been ripped off and I have major side-boob going on.

I shrug. Oh well. At least it's comfortable.

Unbuttoning my jeans, I kick off my shoes and shimmy out of them. My knife falls to the floor catching my attention. I'm sleeping with this knife like a fucking teddy bear tonight.

Turning the light off, I head to the bed and nestle under the worn sheets. They smell of a man, spicy and clean. My thighs clench together in an attempt to smother the ache smoldering between them. It's been awhile since I've gotten laid, and my body has a mind of its own.

Clutching the knife, I close my eyes, my heart beating heavy. How the hell I'm supposed to sleep in a place full of murderers, drug dealers, and possible rapists is a joke.

I could kill Jillian for doing this to me. Then again it is getting me closer to the Outlaws.

FELIX

"The Lost Bastards?" Machete asks surprised after I tell the patched in members the information Alessandra gave me.

"That's what she said," I clarify. The Lost Bastards are a small little bitch club.

"Tomorrow, we retaliate. Make a statement to the surrounding clubs that we are not fucking going anywhere, and we are not taking this shit!" Zeek sneers, his face turning red with the disrespect.

"You," he points at me. "Alessandra is your responsibility, so find out what you can about her pops. Surely someone in our pocket can lead us to something," Zeek orders.

Leaning back in my chair, a cigarette hanging from my mouth, I nod in acceptance.

Looks like I've claimed this bitch without my consent. She's going to hate me until it burns, and then thirst for me until she realizes she starving.

I'm going to enjoy this.

"I don't mind the parties at night, but if you wake up my kids I'm going to put a lug in one of your fucking legs!" He eyes the table. "Also, if you see any of the bitches giving my ol' lady a hard time you better stop that shit in a hurry. I told them if they even looked in her direction they were banned. She is the club's queen now, and everyone better just fucking accept that."

Everyone gives a silent nod, including me.

Zeek slams the gavel down, declaring the meeting over and snapping me back to my memory.

"Oh, and unless you're sleeping in one of the chairs, you'll have to share a room with Alessandra, Felix," Zeek informs last minute, and the rest of the men laugh at my expense as they exit the chapel. I'm not laughing. Not at fucking all.

"I'll take the goddamn chair," I grit.

Not being able to sleep, I sit up. A crick in my neck throbbing down my back. My bare back sweaty and sticking to the leather. Resting my elbows on my knees, I run my hands through my long hair exhausted.

"You okay, baby?" A voice coos from the corner. Glancing up I notice Gia sitting in an adjacent chair with a flannel blanket covering her. The room smells like stale cigarettes and cheap perfume, it's giving me a damn headache.

"Can't sleep," I mutter.

She tosses the blanket off her lap and slides to her knees, sauntering over with hooded eyes. A black Harley shirt hanging off one shoulder, and her hair tossed in a hot mess of a ponytail.

Rubbing her hands up and down my legs she runs her tongue along her bottom lip sexually.

"Want me to help you with that?" she asks huskily, lust thick in her eyes.

Leaning back in the chair, I raise a challenging brow. *Why not?*

Unzipping my jeans, she shoves her hand into my pants and pulls out my cock. Using both hands, she pumps it from the base to tip. Flicking the tip with her tongue, my cock pulses with the temptation. She giggles and runs her tongue along the shaft and my balls squeeze as I grow in her hands. Done with the seductive, flirty act. I grip her by her hair and shove her tonsils first onto my cock. She gags, but gets the point, and starts sucking and slurping. Spit slips down onto my balls as she sucks me like a vise. Leaning my head back on the chair I close my eyes and sigh through gritted teeth. My hand still in her hair I guide her up and down, her hot mouth licks and sucks me into bliss.

Her tits bounce and hit against my knees with every bob, her nipples skipping across them. Using my free hand, I cup her neck, the flesh not as silky as I would like. It's more leathery and worn. Much like the rest of her body.

Blue Bird's strong eyes flash behind my closed eyes from when I had my hand around her throat, ready to squeeze the life out of her.

I shake my head, trying to void her fucking face in this moment. It's no use. My throat bobs, my body tensing as I think about her.

That mouth Blue Bird possesses, that temper, that fucking body. I blow my load into the back of Gia's throat without warning. My dick pulsing with pleasure, my balls squeezing so hard it hurts. Gia chokes, her head flying off my cock.

Opening my eyes, I find her on her hands and knees trying to catch her breath as my cum drips from her lips.

Rage riddles up my spine as I acknowledge I just came to a fucking cop - of all bitches.

Standing I shove my junk back in my pants and strut to my room.

"Where are you going?" Gia asks with a hoarse voice.

I don't answer her because I'm not entirely sure what the fuck I'm doing and it's none of her fucking business.

Opening the door to my room, I close it quietly. My back to the door, I slide my ass to the floor, elbows to my knees as I watch the woman I just blew my load to sleeping in my bed.

She has one of my shirts on, her brown hair all over my pillow as she sleeps peacefully. There's more to this woman than just a cop, I can tell when I look deep in her eyes. The Devil is dancing in those angelic eyes. She's full of temptation and charm and she knows it. I want to know her story, I need to know it. Because right now I'm a fucking hypocrite; busting Zeek's balls for screwing a law enforcement, and I'm over here eye fucking her best friend.

I recognize sin when I look it in the eye. I'm drawn to it, and I'm drawn to Alessandra like a reaper is to an angel. I want to drag her into my world and tear her apart. I hate that I'm like that, but it's what I was raised to do. Destroy, kill, and take no mercy. There is no light in my life, but looking at Alessandra I can see that may be the closest thing I'll ever get to it.

Digging in my pocket, I pull out that joint I rolled earlier and light it. The green herb filling my lungs, and relaxing my racing thoughts instantly.

Alessandra's foot slides up her leg, scratching her bare calf and my dick jumps to attention as if I didn't just get sucked off moments ago. She's awake. My eyes fall on a scar on her lower back, I can't tell what is it. An X maybe.

"Where'd you get the scar?" I ask.

Her shoulders rise.

"First bike ride," she mumbles sleepily. Narrowing my eyes, I find it hard to believe falling off a bike makes that kind of scar. It's so exact and deep. It lures me into her world wanting to know more.

Pulling the blunt away from my mouth I eye the burning cherry, blowing smoke into the dark air.

"What's your dad's name? Give me details," I question with a husky voice. Seconds pass before she rolls over and hits me with those beautiful lost eyes. Her nipples are hard, poking through my shirt. I've seen a lot of posers wear our gear before, but fuck if Alessandra doesn't pull it off perfectly.

Biting my lip, I have to restrain myself from thinking about her grinding on my lap wearing nothing but that shirt. Music from Machete's room can be heard, "Tainted Love" by Marilyn Manson is not helping my sexual need right now.

"His name was Officer Brock Lucas, he was thirty-eight years old when he was killed on the job. They said he was shot before the suspect took his own life. His partner, Officer Kelly, lost it to PTSD and retired. I have no idea where he is, but he reached out recently giving me a dog in the blood line of the department."

Taking another hit, I eye her through the smoke rolling from my blunt.

"And you think there's more to his death why, princess?" I taunt. His demise seems legit to me. Why is she digging up old graves? Boredom? Is she trying to sue the department for money? Wouldn't surprise me, by the looks of her she seems like an uppity bitch.

Her brows furrow, her lip curling with anger. Seems I struck a nerve. She tosses the blankets off her and slides off the mattress. Her long, tanned silky legs catch my attention first. I have a thing for a woman with long tanned legs, it's what attracts me first. Black lace panties play peekaboo with my ripped up shirt and I have to contain the feral growl wanting to escape my mouth.

Taking me by surprise she straddles my lap, plucking the joint from my fingertips she wraps her plush pink lips around the end and inhales a breath so big the joint lights up the small space between us. Her eyes never leave mine, and my heart pounds in my chest. My hands having a mind of their own I can't help but touch the sides of her thighs. God, they're so fucking soft and smooth. She's a vixen hiding behind a toxic badge. She exhales, the smoke dancing upward into the sky and painting the perfect picture, the perfect woman. Dark tangled hair, brown lost eyes, and she's wearing nothing but my shirt as she straddles my lap in black lace panties. She's the good girl gone bad. My kryptonite.

Her brown hair falls in her face, her lips parting as smoke rolls out of her mouth drifting around her like the devil just granted me a wish in return for my soul.

I grip her by the shirt, the sides of her tits showing from the sleeves being ripped off my shirt and pull her close. She's temptation with a price, one I want so fucking badly. She seems unfazed by my aggressive pull as she places the blunt between my lips.

"You know nothing about me," she replies smoothly before sliding off my lap. Making sure to rock against my length before breaking contact fully. "We had a deal, just fucking hold your end up, yeah?" she sasses before climbing back into my bed.

Holy fuck. Placing the blunt back between my lips I inhale a large breath. Watching the bitch that is wearing my shirt, and sleeping in my bed. Pretending to be the good guy when I know for a fact, she's a badass bitch.

I've just met my match.

"Brown 5, you will train harder, fight harder do you *understand?" The man scolds as a jet of cold water pelts against my back. Blood and dirt slip off my raw skin and into a rusty drain as I cling to the wall, crying as the pins and needles of the showerhead spray into me merciless.*

"I tried!" I wail.

"No, you didn't. You showed mercy and backed down, and that kindness will be smothered from you, or I will tear it from you!" he threatens, pounding the water in my face. I gasp, trying to turn my head every which way, my hair matting to my face, I lose where I'm positioned and slip and fall onto the hard tiled floor. My body biting into the cool hardness.

"Stop!" I scream, waking up to the smell of coffee and leather.

It takes me a second to remember where I am as I come to. Then it all replays like a bad movie. My mouth is dry and tastes of bad weed as I climb out of bed and go into the bathroom. I grab the tube of toothpaste off the counter and dab some on my finger and slide it across my teeth, using the pad of my finger as a pretend toothbrush.

I toss the shirt on the unmade bed and dress in the clothes I had on yesterday before stepping out of the room. Machete and his gun aren't standing guard, thank God, so I head into the main area. I smell coffee and hear babies crying. It looks tamer today than what I remember seeing last night.

"Good morning!" Jillian beams from the bar, a cup of coffee sitting in front of her as she soothes a baby in her lap. I look around the club curious how everyone is accepting her being in here but nobody seems to be bothered by it. They are on their phones or watching TV.

A woman with dark long hair is wearing a sling with Layken in her hold. She's more dressed than some of the girls I saw around here last night. An ol' lady perhaps? She's wearing a red flannel shirt tied in the front and dark jeans claiming her thick thighs.

"Want some coffee?" the lady asks, and I realize I've been staring longer than acceptable.

"No thank you. I'll grab a cup at the station," I inform softly. A tight-lipped smile spreads across her aged face and she begins to wipe the counter. I look around again, curious where the girls were from last night that gave me a hard time.

"Where is everyone?" I ask curiously.

"By everyone do you mean the guys or the woman's nose you broke last night?" the woman asks with a snarky tone. My eyes widen, and I suck in a tight breath as Jillian hits me with a surprised look. The lady hits me with warm eyes, a smile pulling at her wrinkled lips. "I'm Carola, I take care of the boys, and I say boys because that's exactly what they are," she smirks, her Italian accent thick. "The skanks that prance around here won't be around during the day out of respect for the ol' ladies," she informs me.

"You broke someone's nose?" Jillian finally asks, and I shrug sheepishly.

"Dolly's to be exact," Carola clarifies.

Jillian looks to Carola and they begin to laugh in unison as if they are good friends. Feeling out of place, and needing a change of clothes I rub my hand up and down my arms.

"I should be going, I work today," I inform Jillian.

"Oh," she seems displeased. "Well, I can have someone escort you—"

"Not necessary. I'll be fine," I interject, needing some space from all of this. She gives me a scolding look, and I sigh heavily. Jillian has really taken to the club, and I'm happy for her but I'm not a club member and feel very out of place here.

"Look honey, you think Zeek protects everyone? That he sends one of his guys to babysit a cop that isn't even one of his member's ol' lady? Because he doesn't." She shakes her head, her thick brows narrowed with disappointment. "You must have done something to earn that respect, now accept it and stop being a bitch," she snaps, and my chest rises with anger.

"That's just the thing, I haven't done anything to deserve it," I retort.

"You're *my* family and that is good enough," Jillian states with hard eyes. Carola points a sharp finger at her.

"There ya go. Family is the biggest bond, and that is something Zeek is trying to pound into his men's code," Carola adds.

Biting my lip nervously, I take in what she's said. I know Zeek is trying to strengthen the brotherhood of his club since he's taken over fully, and I think that's a great thing. However, he's still a criminal and unpredictable. He is the wolf and the fucking leader of the pack. Jillian may trust him, but I don't.

"After work, I will grab some clothes, and check on my

mom and be back here," I reply curtly. "I'll make sure Raven or someone is with me if it makes you happy to know that I'm not alone," I continue.

"It does actually," Jillian replies over the rim of her coffee cup. "I don't need one of your boyfriend's men to tail me," I add, and Jillian scoffs. She's changed, she used to be nothing but a feeble, follow the rules, sheriff. She is darker now, more courage than what is good for her.

Carola pulls a gun out and slides it across the bar, my gun to be exact.

"How'd you get this?" I ask grabbing it.

"Felix said you'd need it," she shrugs.

"I knew I should have brought my flash-bang gun," I mutter. The element of surprise would have had them by the balls.

"You have one of those?" Jillian asks with excitement.

"You don't?" I ask with surprise. Jillian has everything when it comes to carrying a weapon, so I thought.

"A what?" Carola snaps, a look of confusion on her face.

"It's a bra you wear that holsters a gun. You go to flash a guy and bam!" I use my finger and thumb to imitate a gun going off, winking in the process. I've never got to use mine, and am itching to.

"Well I'll be," Carola mumbles in amazement. "I guess it's better than hiding it in your hooch." She shrugs, and Jillian eyes her with wide eyes. The girls that run around here, it wouldn't surprise me what comes out of their hooch. "Anyway, one of the men will collect your mom tonight," she informs casually, and my eyes widen. This is news to me, and surely a fucking mistake.

"Here? They're bringing her here?" I point to the floor, my eyes wide as saucers.

"Yeah, I could use some help now that I'm helping Jillian,

she'll be safe," Carola informs. My eyes fall to Jillian, my mouth wide.

"Was this your idea?"

Jillian shrugs, patting Samuel's back.

"I think it's a really good idea. Your mom will love it."

"My mom is not well, you know that. She will have no idea where she is." My voice comes off more serious than I intend.

"Then there's no problem," Carola clips. I roll my eyes, sliding my gun into my waistband. Unbelievable. Is everyone around here so pushy and controlling?

"See ya tonight," Jillian show-tunes.

"Whatever," I huff. I've lost my best friend to the outlaws. It's official.

FELIX

Pulling up to the Lost Bastards' club we keep the engines running on our motorcycles. Two men are standing outside smoking a cigarette, eyeing us like they're confused. Probably prospects, out of the loop of club business and who their enemy is right about now. The building is made up of worn stucco, and the front door is wide open. A cheap black vinyl banner hangs above the front door displaying the club colors proudly. Glancing at Zeek, I give him the nod, portraying let's do this. Opening my cut, I pull out my AK 47 and like the rest of the boys, we return the decorating favor and spray bullets into their building.

The two men drop to the ground, crawling to cover as we relentlessly empty our clips.

"Hey, hey, hey!" Someone waves a blue bandana from a broken window in an attempt to surrender. I can't help but laugh, what do they think this is? The wild west?

Zeek holds his hand up, halting us from replacing our clips and continuing lighting their ass up. Hands up in the air, no other than Apollo walks out of the front door idiotically unarmed. He's much older than any of our guys. White hair peeks out from under his bandana wrapped around his head that is stained with sweat. Deep wrinkles frame his eye, and mouth, and his white beard gives Santa a run for his game.

"You got three seconds to explain why you attacked my club before I pump a bullet in your skull," Zeek threatens.

"Look man, it wasn't personal it was just business," Apollo states, like that makes up for everything.

"Waking my men up with a drive-by is about as fucking personal as it gets." Zeek tilts his head to the side, his tone edging on irritated.

"Not to mention your weak ass intimidation tactics of spooking his ol' lady," I counter, it had to be one of them who drove by Jillian and Zeek's house.

"Whoa, that wasn't us." He points at me. "I admit, we initiated war with the drive-by, but we didn't stalk down no one's ol' lady," he snorts.

Aiming my gun, finger heavy on the trigger I smirk. "Well, welcome to war with the Outlaws, bitch," I sneer, and lay into the trigger. Zeek and the rest of the men follow suit, firing their weapons. Bodies drop to the ground like flies, the smell of gunpowder and blood thick in the air. Return fire nearly misses us as the Bastards shoot over their shoulder as they run for their life. After the area is cleared of either men who took cover or are dead, we lower our guns.

Coughing up blood Apollo lies on the ground holding his side that is obviously wounded. None of his men running to his aid tells me how much of a club this bullshit MC really is.

Turning my bike off, I put it on the kickstand and walk over to Apollo, Zeek in tow.

Placing my weapon in my holster, I pull out my buck knife and kneel down.

"This is our retaliation, it won't be easy, it won't be fair, and it won't be quick." I place the blade to his neck and his eyes widen.

"Please, let's make a deal," he begs, tears filling his eyes. His hands flinging everywhere to keep me away. Machete grabs his arms and pins them down like something in WWE.

"We only make deals with clubs we recognize, and your bullshit fly by night Boy Scout group is not one," I clip. He wants to play the sinner, but can't handle the monsters that linger in the same hell. He's a fucking poser, who is about to give this city a wake-up call. We are the alpha club, we own this city and have earned it through blood and respect. We will continue to do that, no matter how deep we dig our graves.

"You have someone much higher than you wanting you wiped from Las Vegas, and when that deed is accomplished, I'll meet you in hell," he coughs before spitting blood in my face. Aw, the anger stage when the victim finally realizes he's not talking his way out.

"Save me a seat," I sneer, fisting my knife.

"Do it," Zeek orders the kill.

I slide the blade across his neck before impaling it in his throat and twisting it, his body goes three shades lighter instantly as his life drains on the desert floor. I feel nothing as I take his life. My heart doesn't skip a beat, and my conscious doesn't come to the surface. This is what I was raised to do, protect my club, my president. I've lost count of the souls I've taken to make my club what it is today. I've accepted my darkness and the monster that I've been claimed to be.

Machete howls like a fucking wolf as Apollo pales, his eyes going still.

A couple of motorcycles roar to life grabbing our attention, and jets off into the desert. Machete and Gatz fire their guns in the direction of the running cowards, but they don't hit their target.

"Want me to go after them?" I ask.

Zeek shakes his head. "No, let the word get out that we're not going anywhere."

ALESSANDRA

"We got a 425, caller wasn't sure what she saw, could have been a 413." The dispatch displays. Raven gives me an awkward eye, obviously not sure what the hell the codes mean.

"Possible gun, the witness isn't sure what she heard."

"731, on our way."

"Copy that."

I head toward the outskirts of town. The location on the MDT indicating that the situation is almost out of my jurisdiction. If Jillian were still on the job, she'd race me to it.

"You okay? You look tired," Raven observes.

"Slept at a... friend's place and didn't sleep well," I mutter, narrowing my brows. I hate how observant she is all of the time. "I'm fine." I lift my chin trying to appear unaffected, but I am exhausted.

"I'm sure you are, you're tough," she smiles, before turning to look out the window.

What the fuck does that mean? She doesn't know me.

Pulling up to the scene I instantly notice the motorcycles.

Coming to a complete stop, my heart skips a beat at what the hell I just pulled up on.

"What? What is it?" Raven asks, trying to sit up in her seat to look over the hill.

"Stay here," I order. Undoing my seat belt I notice Raven does the same. "I said fucking stay put!" I point at her, my tone sharp. Her face goes stoic, and she sits back in her seat with a frown.

Closing my door, I head over the hill to get a better look. My shaky hand on my gun, boots thudding against the asphalt I come face to face with a fucking massacre. The building of the Lost Bastards, a graveyard. Sweat drips down my back as I lose my breath. They are bodies everywhere, the smell of bullets and death thick.

One of the Outlaws turns and familiar cold eyes find mine. His hair is in a bun, his leather cut displaying his club's colors. The Sin City Outlaws. Felix pulls a cigarette away from his mouth with bloody hands as he watches me, blowing smoke into the wind. He doesn't seem afraid of me, or concerned at what I'm witnessing. He looks like a beautifully broken savage in blood in leather.

Looking at the blood bath, I suddenly realize this is the club of the Lost Bastards. I did this. I gave Felix the missing puzzle piece to complete his masterpiece of anarchy.

Looking away, I think of my options. I could call this in and for once, The Outlaws have been caught in their game and they could go away for life. I glance back, noticing Zeek talking to one of his men, completely oblivious to me being here. If I turn it in, what does that mean for Jillian and the kids? What does that mean for me if I arrest the man I need Intel from?

Grabbing my radio on my shoulder, I lean toward it.

"731, there- there is nothing here," I choke on my words,

my stomach knotting with alarm at what the fuck I'm doing.

"731, copy that."

Turning away from the scene I head back to my cruiser, my eyes glossy, as I want to cry. My legs feel like weights, and my hands are trembling. My chest feels cold, and I feel like I may vomit any second with what I just did.

"Alessandra!" Felix hollers after me. I don't turn back, I keep my head down and pick up my pace. "Fucking stop!" Felix barks, grabbing my arm and whipping me around to face him.

His wild eyes search mine as the wind wraps around me like a vise, sending a shiver up my spine. His hair is beautiful and spotted with blood, his hands stained with another's life.

"What are you doing here?" he asks gravelly. Swallowing hard I look past him, none of his men looking in our direction.

"I'm not here," I mutter through clenched teeth.

"I just want to make something clear. You weren't here and you saw nothing—"

My head whips in his direction.

"Or what?" I bite out and he steps into my space. His hard stare looking down at me as I glare up at him.

"You get in that fucking car and call this in, they will kill you, do you understand?" he states so seriously my heart skips a beat.

"Why do you care?" I tilt my head to the side. If they kill me, he'd be off babysitting duty.

"Because, they'd send me to do it and I don't want—" He looks away, his Adam's apple bobbing as he swallows. His face is hard, his eyes looking above me.

"Don't want to what?" I push.

"Don't be stupid," he mutters before his sight falls onto mine.

Closing my eyes, I lower my head. "Too late," I whisper. I've already done so much stupid shit that there's no turning back.

"We both have issues Alessandra, but if you do something stupid like try and take us down I'll have to kill you and... that is an issue for me," he points at himself. I scoff, not sure what he means by that.

Opening my eyes, Felix's lips crash against mine, and a buzz of electricity zips through my body as I sway into him. Lost in the world of a convict I almost forget all the death around us until the smell of blood wafts around us mixed with grains of the empty desert. I'm a cop, he'd kill me because that is his code and I need to remind myself of that line. Sinking my teeth into his bottom lip, I bite down hard. He winces and pulls back. Blood drips from his lip as he glares at me with beautifully damaged eyes. His blood stained thumb swiping at his lip I just nailed with my teeth.

"So you like it rough?" he raises a brow, his voice full of arrogance. Rolling my eyes, I turn to walk away, and he smashes his lips to mine again. Brows furrowed I push him hard, and he chuckles at my reaction. Rage fills my chest, this is all just a fucking game to him.

"Don't do something stupid, Alessandra," he hollers, and I raise my hand and flip him off as I continue my walk over the hill back to my cruiser. My heart jackhammers against my chest, my lips tingling where he kissed me. My panties damp from the desire throbbing deep in my core.

I don't know how much longer I can keep my guard up.

The desire to have his beard between my legs is overpowering my badge.

Hands sweaty, mouth dry, I walk away from the biggest bust of not only my career but also the station's.

Climbing inside Raven looks at me with wide eyes.

"Well, what was it?"

"Nothing," I reply softly, sniffling in the snot threatening to drip from my nose I avoid looking at her. Doing a U-turn in the road I head back to the city, avoiding eye contact with Raven the whole time.

We have a saying in my line of work. The criminals are the wolves, the citizens the sheep, and us law enforcement, are the sheep dogs.

My soul was just ripped from my chest by a fucking wolf, and I'll never be the same again.

"You have something," Raven points at my mouth, her brows furrowed. Pulling down my visor I notice blood staining my upper lip. Using the back of my hand I wipe at Felix's blood. His DNA claiming me, marking me and poisoning me all at the same time.

"Nothing, my lips are chapped. The desert and all," I shrug, slamming the visor shut.

FELIX

"What was that?" Mac asks, noticing Alessandra pull away in her cruiser. The red plastic container containing gasoline in hand. I'm not sure what all he just saw, so I shrug and light a cigarette instead of answering him right away. I don't know what compelled me to fucking kiss her but the sting in my lip has my dick harder than a brick, and my gut twisted with guilt that I'm betraying my brotherhood.

"Alessandra," I growl, wiping at my lip to make sure there's no more blood.

"She going to be a problem?" he looks at me with a sideways glance.

"Nah," I shake my head, eyeing the dry blood on my

fingernails.

Flicking my cigarette into the wind, I blow smoke into the air. It lands on a trail of gas leading a path around each of the bodies and into the clubhouse.

"I need you to do some digging for me," I state, not ask.

"What's up?"

"Look into an officer Brock Lucas. He was killed on the job and I want to know if there was some shady shit going down."

"You got it," Mac pats my back, heading back to the SUV. No doubt hitting up his laptop. He loves shit like this, hacking and finding pieces of crap nobody wants anyone to find. He lives for the personal challenge, and arrogantly admits no firewall will keep him out.

"We're done here, let's get before we're seen," Zeek orders, the clubhouse now in full flame.

Black smoke dances into the sky, the fire hot and killing any of our DNA.

"Too late," I whisper, looking in the direction of where Alessandra was last.

Sitting at the counter nursing a beer, I scratch at the blood under my nails. Replaying everything that happened today. *Will clubs back off knowing we can handle our shit without the mafia? Will Alessandra talk about what she saw?*

"Hey, I got some information on that officer," Mac says excitedly as he slides up next to me.

Not sure if Jillian is around I stand and head to the room we have church in, Mac following.

"First off, there are no birth records for Alessandra Lucas, so I looked into the adoption agencies only to find her dad is not her real dad. Brock's record with the department has many write-ups as he didn't follow the rulebook. As for the day he died," Mac shakes his head. "I couldn't find shit, not even the name of the suspect that was shot. Someone didn't want anyone to find this shit man. His partner's statement doesn't match what happened at the scene," Mac explains with a conflicted look.

"So he wasn't shot?"

"I don't know, his partner is the only one that knows," Mac continues.

"So we need to find the partner that disappeared." I take a sip of my beer.

"Two steps ahead of you," Mac says, typing into his computer before turning the screen around. Looks like he's residing in the ghetto about an hour from here.

"You up for a little ride?" I ask.

"We ain't looking for trouble, man," Mac shakes his head. "Just information."

I laugh, setting my beer down. "Well that's no fun." I'm always looking for trouble, the adrenaline rush is what guides me through my darkest days.

Zeek struts into the chapel with white shit on his shoulder. Mac jumps out of his seat pointing at him.

"What the fuck is that?"

Zeek looks down, before brushing it off like it's nothing.

"Puke... I think," Zeek mumbles.

"Looks like bird shit," I silently laugh.

"Or like you just jerked off and couldn't find your load!" Mac raises a brow, keeping a safe distance from Zeek.

"There is something seriously wrong with you." I tilt my beer toward Mac.

"I need to get my hands dirty, go for a ride or something.

This domestic shit is starting to get to me," Zeek groans.

"Well you're in the right place because I'm looking for a little trouble," I smile with a shit-eating grin.

FELIX

Driving to the address Mac gave us, we end up in the ghetto. It's a shitty neighborhood for a retired cop.

We pull up to a house that is missing siding, has a broken window at the very top, and shingles are missing from the roof. There's a black Buick in the driveway that is chipped and has tape holding plastic over the back window.

"You sure this is the address?" I ask pulling my helmet off. My hair gets caught in it and I have to untangle it. I swear I should cut this shit, but the chicks seem to love it.

"Yeah, this is it," Mac replies confidently.

Throwing my leg over my seat I notice the neighbors eyeing us suspiciously. They look like crack heads. Skinny, thin dull hair, and dark bags under their eyes. Their house matches Kelly's in upkeep. I jut my chin at them, and they look away quickly. Respect, it feels good.

Machete knocks on the front door, and nobody answers. He knocks again and I notice the curtain move in the bay window located at the front of the house.

"He's in there," I state.

"Kelly?" Zeek shouts. "We need to talk."

Suddenly a bullet clips through the front door, snagging Machete in the arm. He hisses, grabbing at the bloody wound.

Not fucking around, I kick the door open. It slams into Kelly knocking him on his ass, his gun skidding along the dirty floor.

He reaches for the gun, and I slam my boot into his face as hard as I can. Busting his nose, I can feel the crack beneath my foot.

Zeek grabs the gun, and Machete stomps into the house and grabs Kelly by the stained shirt before laying a series of punches to his face. His strength more than he knows, he's about to kill the motherfucker.

"Easy brother, we still need him alive for information." I try and hold him back. Machete is a machine that can't be controlled unless he wants to be controlled.

Machete breathes heavily, eyeing Kelly like dinner before tossing his limp body to the dirty floor. Machete wipes the blood from his arm, and smears it across Kelly's face. Kelly cringes, his face painted like something from an Indian movie as it marks under his eyes and forehead.

Machete growls, holding his arm as he glares at a whimpering Kelly.

Kelly wipes his face of the blood, scooting to his ass. His eyes are wide with fear, his bottom lip trembling as blood slips from the bridge of his nose down his chin.

"You look like you've seen a ghost," I imply, tilting my head to the side.

"You guys. It was you guys who did this to me!" he sobs, and I furrow my brows in confusion.

"What? Broke your nose?" I shrug. "Because you kind of had that coming with your shitty hospitality." It smells like body odor and pizza in, the house has no lights and looks trashed.

"It was your kind that took my partner from me!" He points

with a shaky hand. "You took my life!" he continues hysterically.

Zeek grabs a chair from the table and sits in it casually, and Mac raids the man's kitchen like he normally does. I swear Mac is a bottomless pit when it comes to eating.

"Tell us what you know about Alessandra and her father," Zeek demands with a no bullshit tone.

Kelly sits up straighter, sniffling in blood, his eyes watering from the pain. His hair is greasy and unruly, his beard outgrown and disgusting. He looks like a bum.

"What about them?" he replies vaguely.

Having enough of the games, I raise my gun to his head, the chamber clicking.

"I'm about three seconds from blowing your fucking brains out if you don't tell me what I want to know!" I threaten. I can feel Zeek staring at me, knowing he's not impressed with my impatience or attitude.

"Okay! Okay!" Kelly raises his hands, his body stiff as I might pull the trigger any moment.

"Brock found her in this place held underground. There were fifteen kids of all ages and genders. Investigators conveyed the missing children were taken from tourists and used for training purposes. Take a kid, train them to fight and kill," he explains. "It was The Sin City Outlaws little army if you ask me!" he spits, and I snarl with that inaccurate assumption.

"What the fuck does that mean?" Zeek sneers.

"Cross! He was in charge of the whole operation, and everyone knew it!" Kelly informs with a shaky voice.

I glance at Zeek with wide eyes, this is news to us that Cross was running an underground operation like that. "We found parents to several of the kids, but a few of them didn't know their names, hell, they didn't even know their birthdays they were taken so young. Alessandra was one of the ones who didn't know anything about herself. Told Brock her name was Brown 5." He begins to laugh hysterically, and it unnerves me. "She didn't know her name, but knew how to break someone's neck, and shoot a gun at age five. How ironic," he snorts.

"Jesus Christ," Zeek mumbles, rubbing his chin.

"Cross was of course cleared of all charges because none of the kids actually saw him, just heard his name. We had one witness, but they went missing, and so Cross walked free, nobody was fucking charged for what happened to those kids!" Kelly begins to cry, his back and forth of emotions telling me he might be high.

"What happened to Brock?" I ask, biting my inner cheek.

"Cross found out that Brock adopted one of his prodigies. Brock's dying wish was that Cross let Alessandra go and Cross said she was tainted goods anyway and ended his life right in front of me before killing one of his own men to cover it up. He was going to kill me but I ran, and I've been hiding ever since." The man looks up at us with sad eyes. Tears slip from his eyes, but I'm unmoved. "I'm a coward," he wails before grabbing the barrel of my gun and pressing his temple into it. "Just kill me!" he spits through gritted teeth.

I jerk my gun from his head and grab him by the hair making him look me in the eyes.

"The Sin City Outlaws were not a part of that charade, I assure you," I tell him before tossing him back on his ass.

"You're going to want to see this, brother," Mac states to no one in particular from another room, his voice laced with shock. My gut twists, not liking the sound of this.

"Keep an eye on him," I tell Machete, and follow Zeek and Mac into the living room. The couch is covered in plastic, and the coffee table is littered with crack and foils.

On the wall are pictures of Alessandra of all ages, plastered like a collage of a serial killer's wet dream. Her at the gym, park, with Jillian, and us. It's stalking to a whole other level.

"This is some sick shit," Zeek mutters, pulling one of the photos of Jillian and Alessandra down. They're laughing together at what looks like a diner.

Right in the middle of all the photos, is one of a little brown haired girl and man in a cop uniform. Alessandra's dad I presume. Pulling it from the wall, I stuff it in my cut.

My spine feels stiff, my stomach sick. Striding into the hallway, I eye Kelly who has obviously gone off the deep end. PTSD, or some shit. My hands flex with an unknown urge I can't pinpoint. Jealousy? Rage? I don't like that he has been watching her without her knowing. Some of those photos were of her dressing, and I know she's not mine but knowing what I do, I feel like I know her more than she knows herself. I have a responsibility to keep her safe now.

"Stay away from Alessandra," I warn him. Head lowered, eyes hooded I silently tell him the pain I will inflict him if he so much as looks her way. He shakes his head, sniffling and rocking back and forth.

"No, she needs my protection, especially from you! Your kind ruined her life, and mine, remember!" he shouts, a blood vassal protruding from his forehead. "She needs protection from herself," he mumbles, before pulling at his hair and rocking like a madman.

Alessandra isn't as innocent as anyone thinks, she's a darker breed and I'm wanting to get to know her more and more with every piece to her puzzle I find out.

"He's fucking lost it, and a liability," I tell everyone. Pulling my gun from my holster I point it at him and fire a bullet right into his skull. Blood and brain matter paint the wall behind him as his head falls to his chest.

"Goddamn it, Felix," Zeek scorns me.

"Needed to be done," I insist, tucking my gun in my pocket. If anyone was a danger to Alessandra it was him, and I'll be damned if anyone stands in my way of Alessandra. If I want her, I will have her.

"We need to get out of here, and fast," Mac insists, looking out the window.

"Machete, make sure the neighbors are aware they didn't see shit," Zeek orders, his tone indicating the bodies will pile up if they say a word. "Clean that blood off his face with bleach too, last thing we need is fucking DNA on the body," Zeek scorns.

"I'll just torch the place." Machete shrugs like it's no big deal.

"Fucking fire bug," Zeek shakes his head.

Stepping out of the house I inhale a sharp breath. The smell of the air is mixed of gunpowder and metallic.

Why did I kill him? Why do I care?

The questions run through my head like a bad memory.

Taking one step at a time down the porch I can't help but want to protect Alessandra now. It was an obligation at first, and now my priority.

It's no wonder I'm attracted to Alessandra, she doesn't have blue blood running through her like she thinks. She's much darker, and our inner beasts are speaking to one another without us even knowing it. It all makes sense now.

Knowing the information I do, there is no stopping me from taking what I want.

ALESSANDRA

Driving to my house, I hear the familiar sound of a motor-cycle. Slamming the driver side door shut Felix pulls into my driveway and cuts the engine.

"What are you doing here?" I ask.

"Taking you back to the club. Where you belong." He raises a challenging brow. Jesus, they just won't give up will they.

"Don't you think this is a little ridiculous, nobody is coming after me." I look around the block to indicate my point. It's empty, and as pristine as the Brady Bunch.

"Just following orders, sweetheart," he smarts, and I roll my eyes.

"Yeah, you look like a rule-following kind of guy," I mumble low enough he can't hear me.

Turning on my heel I head inside the house.

"Ma?" Nobody answers. I wonder if they already came and got her?

The door shuts behind me and Felix stands there. His eyes are darker than normal, his stare unfamiliar. His big shoulders flex as he crosses his arms, his stance wide. He takes up my whole living room, and looks powerful. I've never brought a man home before, not that I invited this one.

"Get your shit," he orders. "I ain't got all day."

"Asshole," I mutter.

Pete571 runs into the room with his tongue hanging out of his mouth and ears flopping. He's excited to see me, and is running at full speed.

"Whoa!" Felix tenses, pulling his gun out and aiming at Pete. The way he holds his gun, the look on his face I instantly have to clench my thighs to stifle the throbbing. You can tell a lot about a man by the way he handles his gun.

Out of instinct, I step in front of his aim, my hands raised.

"NO!"

Felix flicks his gaze to me before back at the dog. "Put the gun down, he's just a dog!" I demand. My arms raised in the air I take notice of how Felix's eyes rake down my body slowly, it does things to me.

"Not *just* a dog, these motherfuckers eat my kind. They're fucking fur-missiles," he insists. Lowering his gun, he raises his pant leg and a set of teeth marks scar his calf. I laugh, bending down to pick up my dog. I still need to find a name for him besides Pete571. He won't be a department issued dog, he will be my family.

"Well, you know they're just teaching idiots not to run one bite at a time," I wink, trying my hardest not to laugh at Felix and his fear of German Shepherds.

"Not funny," he sneers. But it is.

Setting Pete571 down, I go pack a small bag. Making sure to grab clean clothes and my toothbrush.

"Did you find anything out about my dad?" I ask lightly.

"Um, I'm still looking into it, but I can say he's not your dad," Felix tells me.

"I already know that part," I inform with a deep sigh, hearing it confirmed doesn't make it sit any easier though. I wonder how my dad would have told me. How I became his? There's a lot of questions I want to ask him and can't.

Scooping up Pete571, I bite back my emotions.

"I'm ready."

Felix looks at me with a cold expression.

"That dog is not coming to my club."

I raise a brow.

"If he doesn't, then I don't."

Riding on the back of the motorcycle, my bag is tied to the

back, and Pete571 is in my lap. His face is in the wind, and wet tongue hanging out. If I wouldn't know any better, I'd say he has a little biker in him.

Felix shifts between my thighs, reminding me of his strong body between my legs, and my heart bucks at the same time my sex pulses with need. My hands want to run across his back, and up his strong shoulders. To feel his lips against my ear, and his hand in my hair. I wonder if he's a gentle lover, or a ravaging one. Taking every breath with a bite of pain, or caressing and caring. Closing my eyes, I try to control my body's reaction to this man, my shaded thoughts that run rampant. It's no use though. Felix makes me vulnerable when he's near, making a part of myself I knew was there but masked, rise like a welcomed demon. I can't defend myself against what's inside of me around Felix and that scares me. All of this scares me. Whatever it is.

Arriving at the clubhouse, Felix parks his bike, and helps me off. The way his eyes rake me from top to bottom doesn't go unnoticed. My skin prickles beneath his intrusive stare. Looking deep in his eyes you can tell he's lethal and dangerous, but it's laced with something softer than before. Tilting my head to the side I wonder what's changed. There's something there that wasn't there before in the way he looks at me.

Tearing his gaze from mine, he grabs my bag and throws it over his shoulder before strutting toward the clubhouse without a word. Pete571 in my hands I follow in tow. Walking in the clubhouse Jillian's eyes light up at the dog. She runs over to it and instantly squishes his face.

"Oh my God, where did you get him?" she coos.

"Um, he was in the bloodline of my father's K9," I tell her

softly. Her eyes lift to mine in knowing. I look away, not liking the vulnerability I suddenly feel.

"Where are the babies?" I ask, noticing I don't hear a screaming child.

"They're down for the night," she explains with relief.

"What the hell is that?" Machete asks, stepping toward me. He's such big man he could play for the NFL. A fucking lumberjack at best. His red hair is everywhere, his piercing eyes laid right on Pete571. Maybe bringing him wasn't the best idea.

"A dog," I clip.

Machete looks at me before Pete. Then a big smile breaks his serial killer look as he pets his brown fur.

"Never been up close to a German Shepard that isn't trying to eat my face off," he chuckles, and a nervous laugh racks my chest. Machete doesn't do a lot of talking. He seems to be the most brooding, mysterious one around here. If anyone scares me, it's him. "What's his name?"

"Um, they call him Pete571—"

"Oh, we have to rename him. He ain't no police dog. Look at em', he looks like an outlaw." He grabs Pete571 under the arms and lifts him from my hold without warning. Holding him up in the air like a scene from *The Lion King* he looks him over. "Yeah, look at him," he mutters under his breath, admiring Pete. "His name is Rocky," he says with force. He cuts me a hard look as if I better agree. I hold my hands up in surrender, only an idiot would disagree with a man like Machete.

"Rocky it is," I nod. It's better than Pete that's for sure.

The rest of the patched members surround Machete, all talking and cooing over the German Shepherd. All but Felix that is. He's leaning against the bar counter eyeing me with that look again. Like he hates me, but secretly wants me.

"Don't mind him," Jillian whispers in my ear. "Zeek told me a K9 was brought in by the FBI and Felix covered for his dad to escape, only to have his dad killed by a rival gang that same night. I think he blames himself."

I turn where I stand looking at Jillian with panicked eyes. "You're fucking with me?" I ask, I hope.

She gives a sympathetic smirk. "That's what I was told."

Hanging my head, I suddenly feel like a bitch for bringing Pete571, er, Rocky. But what was I supposed to do? Leave him at the house. My stepmom left him when she went to June's, a puppy can't just be left unattended.

"Relax, he'll get over it. He's just playing the brooding biker," she sasses. Taking my gaze from her to him, he's a sight to behold. His elbows are on the bar, his hooded eyes focused solely on me. Those thick lashes and broken eyes hold me where I stand, and I suddenly become aware of my every breath as I stare back. "If I didn't know any better, I'd say those are fuck me eyes," Jillian jeers, before sashaying off down the hall like a know-it-all.

Crossing my arms, I inhale a breath.

I hope Felix doesn't come on to me. I'm too much of a slut to say no to such a sexy man.

Brooding, bad boy, damaged. He's a wet dream. One I'd like to cuff and show him who's in control.

"Brock, baby?" The familiar voice of my mother catches my attention by the bar. She's wearing a baby blue shirt and gray sweatpants, her hair everywhere.

"Mom?" Oh my God, they did bring her here.

She walks up to Mac, her cheeks rosy red as she bats her eyes at him.

"I'm Mac, Mrs. Lucas," Mac insists, a look of worry crossing his handsome face.

My stepmom doesn't seem to care as she grabs Mac's hands.

"Dance with me, it's been forever since you've danced with me," she coos, and Mac sighs before giving in and dancing with her. I start to say something but then shut my mouth. I have no words.

"Oh yeah, your mom is here and keeps thinking Mac is your dad," Jillian informs.

"Shoot me now," I run my hands down my face, and Jillian laughs.

"Hey, she's safe here, and Carola loves her. They're bunking together even."

Pinching the bridge of my nose I nod, trying to see this as a good thing but this is all happening so quickly I can't decide how I feel. I guess she'll be better here than a nursing home, she won't be eating Manwich right out of the can, and maybe keeping her busy helping around here will help with her straying episodes.

"All right, give her the damn dog back," Zeek barks, and Rocky is suddenly shoved in my arms.

"He can stay, but he shits you're cleaning it up," Zeek informs. He eyes me with softer eyes than I've ever seen Zeek process. I wonder if it's because he knows what I saw today?

"Yeah, or Bomber Jack can lick it up," Gatz jokes, elbowing the prospect in the chest and the rest of the guys cackle and laugh.

"I'm going to take him to my room," I reply, noticing the crowd starting to get hectic with the dark hours. It's probably best if I tuck in for the night.

In my room, Rocky is asleep by my side as I listen to the music gently pounding through the walls. It's starting to get wild out there. The smell of cheap perfume and cigarette smoke creeping its way from under my door as the night tires on. I'm not tired, not the least bit. Curiosity has me wanting to explore the nightlife of The Sin City Outlaws. I'm intrigued how wild they get. It's no lie I like good music, good beer, and a good time. Just because I'm a cop, doesn't mean I have to be a nun.

Sitting up on the bed, Rocky's ears perk as his eyes snap to attention.

"Should I go check it out? Maybe just look?" I bite my nails nervously, staring down at Rocky. "I could lie and say I'm getting a drink or something?" Rocky tilts his head to the side, eyeing me like he has no idea what I'm talking about. Jesus, I'm talking to a dog. What has my life come to.

Throwing the blankets off me, I tiptoe to the door and open it. The smell of drugs is strong and sound of "Back In Black" by AC/DC is playing.

A half naked girl saunters down the hall, her hair is puffy with too much hair spray. She's wearing a leather jacket and chaps. I've never seen her before. She slurs something at me, her eyes looking me up and down like I'm the help or something before entering a room at the end of the hall.

Biting my cheek, I fluff my hair a little and look down at my attire. White shirt from the academy, and gray shorts. Shit.

Crossing my arms to cover the logo of the academy, I slip out. I'm just going to look anyway so there is no need to doll up. The hallway is dark, and a couple I don't recognize is making out against the wall. He has one hand up her shirt, and the other down her pants. She looks bored as she plays on her phone.

Stepping past them I enter the mouth of the main action.

Girls dance on the bar, and men staring up at them like they're dancing from heaven. There's two men wrestling by the door that I don't recognize, and a girl just sniffed coke off the tip of Mac's dick. His tongue is sliding along the bottom of his lip as he watches her, his hand firmly on his shaft. He's thick from what I can see. It's thrilling to see, I've never seen anyone let loose like this before. Because I am law enforcement most people keep it tame at parties I'm invited to, scared I'll turn them in or something. My heart thunders at the wild scene unfolding in front of me. Like an adult pop-up book, everywhere you turn there's something else jumping at you that takes you by surprise.

Everyone looks like they're having a good time, and I want to have a good time. I want to be a part of the wild that isn't afraid of me! I don't want to be tucked away in bed like a fucking grandma.

Pushing through the crowd with my mind made up, I head back to my room to change. My eyes catch a glimpse of Gia dancing topless on a man's lap. She has a big rack for such a tiny girl. Bigger than mine that is for sure. Taking a step further toward my room I notice she's not dancing for just any man, it's Felix. His eyes slowly drift from her, to mine and I hold my breath. His hair is pulled up with strays falling into his dark eyes. His jaw ticks, as his hands slide up the back of Gia. I quickly avert my eyes downward, taking a deep breath into my burning lungs. Making quick work of my feet I return to my room.

Tossing my shirt and shorts to the floor, I empty my bag in hopes I have something halfway decent. It won't be biker apparel, but maybe I grabbed something a little sexy.

Grabbing a silky pair of red underwear, I notice they're too big to be panties and unfold it. It's a skimpy dress I bought a long time ago. I never wore it because Jillian said it if you can fold it up and put it in your purse, it's not a dress.

Perfect.

I slide it over my body, the thin silk material painting my body perfectly. I toss my hair over my shoulder and spray some of my perfume on my collarbone. Heading to the bathroom, I pull open my makeup and apply a little dark eye shadow.

The bedroom door opens and shuts and Rocky whines from the bed. Mascara in my hand I continue to apply it to my eyelashes when a bare-chested Felix steps into the reflection of the mirror.

His chest is so chiseled and defined. Tattooed and hard, I bite my lip as I look down, anywhere but at the beast behind me. He's obviously claimed by Gia, and I'm not one to mess with someone else's man.

"Where do you think you're going?" he asks, his voice husky. I lower my mascara wand and frown at his tone.

"What? You can go have a skank ride your lap, but I can't get my rocks off?" I sneer. His jaw ticks, his hands balling into fists. "You got it all wrong if you think I'm going to sit in here and play the good girl while you all have a good time," I laugh, continuing applying my makeup.

In one large step, he's suddenly behind me, his hand striking out and fisting my hair harshly. I whimper, dropping my makeup. My eyes snapping to his. I'm not afraid, not at all. In fact, my nipples bud to attention and my clit pulses with excitement at the control Felix is dominating. A change of pace for me as I'm usually the one in control.

"Maybe you forgot, but I forbid you to open those legs to any of my men," he grits into the back my hair.

"Didn't forget, just don't care," I seethe through the pain

slicing through my scalp. His eyes flash with licks of heat, his left brow lifting. Thrusting his hips against my ass, my eyes nearly roll into the back of my head from the bulge pushing against me. Running his nose behind my ear, he smells me and my mouth parts to allow the hard breath burning in my chest to escape. He's like a feral animal smelling his prey just before he tears into it, and for some reason that has me dripping wet with anticipation.

"Aren't you with Gia?" I breathe heavily. His eyes snap to mine in the mirror.

"I belong to no one," he retorts with hostility.

He kicks my legs apart, his knee pressing into my heat. It takes all my strength not to grind myself onto him. My mouth parts with a rush of sexual needs pulsing through me. "When you're in my house, I say who you fuck," he whispers darkly. "Do you understand?"

"Yes," I whisper through clenched teeth. My eyes glaring at a man that is more than he lets on, one that comes off as a beast, but just might be something softer that only I can see.

He brushes the nape of my neck and the hairs on the back of my neck stand on end, my body wound tight as I white knuckle the sink.

"Did it terrify you when you kissed me?" I ask, and my lips suddenly ache to touch his again.

His chest rises with one steady breath, his hair falling to his menacing eyes.

"Not as much as this," he growls.

He swirls his knees against my clit to grab my attention and a quick gasp wracks my body.

"Jesus," I moan, my fingers gripping the counter for strength.

Crooking my head to the side, he runs his soft lips along the shell of my neck. Goosebumps lick up my arms, a shiver running down my back.

"Jesus can't help you now, Dirty Bird. You're in the den of the Outlaws, and you're mine right now." His words are threatening but promising, sexy but hateful.

I want it all.

He whips me around, my hair flinging in my face. He grabs the thin material of my dress and fists it like Tarzan just before he tears it apart like a goddamn napkin. My breasts bounce freely, my nipples hard and aching for his touch. My bold act of not wearing any panties giving him the full view of my waxed pussy.

His eyes trail down my body agonizingly slow. His expression not giving away that he likes what he sees or not, I squirm under his intrusive stare.

Tucking his bottom lip in between his teeth he trails a finger from my collarbone down between my breasts, slowly to my belly button. My stomach trembles from the soft but ample touch. As if I'm something he's never seen or touched before but has been dying to.

"Are you sure you want to cross that line?" I breathe heavily. His eye snap to mine, and narrow in on me. The forbidden desire that was once a slow ember now an inferno.

"If you're going to be a slut, you're going to be one with me. Understand?" he insults.

"I'm nothing like Gia," I snap. I'm not a slut, I mean, not that he knows of anyway.

Dipping his hand lower his finger brushes over my mound and my body bucks against him.

"Oh I know, trust me. I fucking know," he replies wolfishly. He flicks my clit and my whole body heats to a level I've never known it was capable of.

"I'm going to have this pussy dripping so wet that you're not going to care if I put it in your ass, your mouth, or this sweet little pussy. As long as you have my dick inside of you," he states arrogantly.

My head falls back, my body grinding on its own accord against his hold.

"I thought you didn't fuck cops?" I moan.

He releases his hand from my clit and grabs me by the throat, his face inches from mine. A rush of something exciting and dark races through me with his hard grip around my throat. It angers me but fuels me. I melt into his hold, granting him claim of my entire being. My world spins, and I clench my eyes shut trying to make sense of my body's reaction.

"You're no fucking cop," he seethes, and I can't help but look at him with a lost look. He always sneers at me in disgust that I'm a cop, what's different now?

"Why do you say that?" His eyes flick between both of mine.

"You would have turned us in today if you were." He tilts his head to the side. "Why didn't you?"

I swallow, his hold tight on my throat. "I don't know," I whisper honestly. I have plenty of excuses as to why I didn't, but none of them justify why I really did it. I don't know why I turned around, something inside of me told me to push my feet to turn around and I did. Something dark and dangerous dwelling deep within my soul told me to look away.

Letting go of my throat he grabs me under the thighs, using one hand he clears the counter in reckless abandon of my makeup and toothbrush. All of it flinging around the bathroom.

He plows my ass on the counter, and like a crazed animal, I lose control. Done with the games, done with what is right and wrong. My mouth smashes against his as my hands make work of his belt.

He tastes of weed and whiskey, his lips are hard and demanding. His tongue taking no mercy as it explores my mouth. He pulls a condom from the back pocket of his jeans and rips it open with his teeth. My pussy throbs with what's to come. Using my feet, I push his jeans and underwear just down his ass and his length springs free. It's big in girth and long in length. It's veiny, and the head is massive. My body tingles looking at it. He sheathes his cock in the condom. Setting each of my feet on the edge of the counter I widen my legs for him, giving my pink, wet pussy to him fully. He rests his hand on my collarbone again and stills. His eyes on mine. It's a moment that neither of us speak but something soft and sentimental passes silently.

My nostrils flare in this moment, my heart drumming against my chest.

Using his free hand, he holds the base of his hard length and slams it into my wetness.

My head falls back against the mirror as a satisfying moan erupts from my lips. He stretches me like no man I've been with. His length hits the back of me and fills me fully. It feels so fucking good and hurts just the same. I could fuck him all night.

"Goddamn," he moans, his hand tightening around my throat. The control he seeks turns me on more than I ever thought I'd enjoy. I want it, I crave it. It makes me feel safe watching his strength and dominance take over. He pumps into me again, and I swear the breath is thrust from my lungs. My mouth gaped open, eyes rolled back he hits me just right.

He plunges into me again and again. A jerk of his hips taking my breath away each time. Our impulsive touches, and harsh breathing the closest feeling to having my soul ripped from my chest as he fucks me into a darker realm. His head falls into the crook of my neck, his breath hot and sticky against my skin. His hand remains on my neck, as he owns my whole body telling me who's in charge.

My nails scrape at his back for purchase as I ride the wave of this beast of a man. With a sharp jerk of his hips my back thrusts into the mirror so hard it cracks it, the sound of glass splintering beneath me. But we don't stop or slow down. Nothing can stop us from crossing that forbidden line that both of us have been craving since we met. It's filled with hate, and lust swirled with infatuation and sin. He fucks me hard, and oh so good. Pressure builds in my core, and my toes curl around his back.

My head falls forward, and in a haze I see a blurry image standing in the room behind Felix. I blink and notice it's a fuming Gia. Angry eyes watch us, her chest rising and falling. I smile like the fucking Devil as I ride Felix's cock. Shaking her head, she turns quickly and leaves, making sure to slam the door hard. Felix's body tenses in my hold, and teeth clamp down on my shoulder so hard it's the last ingredient to throw me into ecstasy. I come so hard I see stars and lose my breath. My body wound up so tight I feel like I may combust on this counter.

He pumps his hips one more time, as he stills in my hold. Both of us gasping for air as we come down from our high.

He pulls from the crook of my neck, and eyes me warily. Our bodies are sweaty, and my limbs ache. His chest is flushed, and I can't help but run my nails down his chest like a feral cat. I didn't want this to end, I want more.

"I didn't hurt you did I?" he asks, his tender tone doing things to me.

I shake my head. "No, just the opposite," I smile. I've never had it that rough before, and I loved it. Of course I don't go into detail in telling him that, I don't want to come off like a clinger.

Pulling the condom off his cock, cum drips on the counter. He dabs his finger in it and runs it across my chest like a barbarian. I eye him like a crazy person.

"You don't fuck any of my men, do you understand?" his tone sharp, grabbing his jeans he pulls them up and steps back. That moment of softness gone, and control and dominance back in its place.

"Why? Because you want me for yourself?" I prod. He stops, looking over his shoulder but not quite all the way. The look in his eyes tells me he's battling with what he's about to say.

"I don't fuck cops," he sneers.

My mouth drops, rage fueling my chest so hard I feel my heart tear apart.

"If you think I'm just one of those girls you can control and walk over, then you have another thing coming, asshole!"

That grabs his attention because he turns around and grabs me under the thighs lifting me from the counter. He tosses me on the bed and hovers over me. His fists pressed into the mattress with execution.

"I'm always up for a challenge, Black Bird." I tilt my head at his nickname. He used to call me Blue Bird. "If I see you so much as look at one of my brothers in a manner that pisses me off, I will strip you where you stand and fuck you in front of them all." My thighs clench imagining that scene play out.

"You wouldn't," I dare. He raises a brow, his hair that escaped his man bun falling in his face.

"You seem to think I give a shit, I don't. I'm not a gentleman, don't fool yourself into thinking otherwise," he counters. I furrow my brows at what he thinks of himself.

"Why do you think you're such a bad guy?"

Lowering his head, I instantly feel him cool beneath my hand, his body tensing. He pulls away from me, his hand running through his messy hair.

"Since I was a kid I've lived in the shadows of a motorcycle club. Being the child of A Sin City Outlaws, you're immediately judged as the city's vile underside before you're even allowed to decide your worth. After so many years, you become the thing people say you are," he states so huskily my hearts pangs for him. His eyes meeting mine with darkness and longing. I see then and there not what this man is capable of, but of the beast inside of him, that makes that possible.

"Don't give me that fucking look," he orders, and I pull the sheet over my bare body.

"What look?"

"Like you feel bad for me or something. You and I aren't so different, you're a wolf in a sheep's disguise," he states so calmly, so deeply, and raw it makes me think he knows me more than I know myself for a second. He's implying I'm more savage than I let on. Am I?

Maybe he's talking about what I did today when I turned away from the bloody scene I stepped upon. My eyes shoot to his, what if he found something out about my dad that I don't know about?

"Did you find something out I need to know?" I whisper, my brows furrowing. My heart drumming with hope that he has the piece to this missing puzzle that escapes my soul.

His jaw ticks, his Adam's apple bobbing as he looks away from me. That hardness that he bestows so beautifully but fearfully masking his softer side.

"No, nothing," he replies, pushing off the bed. Grabbing the door handle, he stops where he stands.

"Don't fucking leave this room!" he snaps angrily before

shutting the door with force.

I feel vulnerable and I don't like it. Guilt pangs at my chest at what just happened in that bathroom, how I became so weak to his advance. Hell, I didn't even play hard to get.

Biting my lip his words echoes in my head.

"We're not so different." The way he said it, it had meaning behind it.

My senses tell me he's lying about something. I'm trained to know when someone is lying to me and he just hit every check mark.

FELIX

Stepping outside of the bedroom I rub at my neck anxiously. This feeling running through me unnerves me. I lost control and fucked her, and I felt so close to her, so raw and real that it has me confused and fucking angry. I fucked a goddamn cop. Being inside of Alessandra was like fucking for the very first time. She was soft, smelled good, tight around my cock. I hate her and want her all in one emotion. Running my hands down my face, I exhale a ragged breath. What the fuck did I just do? I betrayed my blood, my fucking code of life. I lose control and I knew I would eventually. Every time I'm near her, it's as if my body is drawn to her regardless of the shiny fucking badge she wears. I want to rip it off and slam my dick into her until she screams every time I see her ass in that cruiser.

"You smell like her."

Looking to my left, Gia is leaning against the wall just outside my door, her arms crossed. Her left brow is raised, her eyes looking at me with judgment. She knows, and I have no doubt will make a fucking mess of things.

"What are you doing here?" I ask, ignoring her accusation. Slipping off the wall like a black widow, she sashays toward me.

"I came to find you, and maybe play a little." She tilts her head to the side as she rubs her hand over my dick. I raise a brow at her and find her tacky rather than sexy for the first time. What is happening to me?

I run my palm down my face, not sure what this fucking means. I fucked a cop, even if she is dirty and has a black past, I'm no good for her. I'll take her into the throes of hell, and won't let her escape. That is why I can't tell her about her past because then our demons really will bond and there will be no turning back. She needs to find out if she wants to play on the dark side or twirl in the light all on her own, and I'm not going to make it easy for her to pick a side. This life is not for little girls.

"Give me five minutes," I growl, shoving past Gia. She giggles annoyingly, and I head into the main area for a shot of whiskey. Needing something to calm my racing thoughts and unfamiliar feelings drumming through my cold veins.

Going behind the bar I grab the whiskey bottle, tossing the cap on the bar I decide to just take three large gulps and say fuck the shot glass.

It burns so good all the way down, instantly warming my blood. My fingers so close to my face I can smell Alessandra's sweet pussy on my fingers. I can't help but inhale a deeper breath, and it pisses me off I want more.

I broke a code being with her, and I liked it. I fucking liked it!

Lowering the bottle, I watch Gia enter a random room down the hall. I need her. I need Gia to ground me, remind me of what I am and this is as good as it gets for me.

Trashy women, breaking the law, and reigning repercussions on the citizens of Vegas. I'm biker trash, and always will be.

Slamming the bottle down, I push past the crowd and right into the room with Gia. She's standing in the middle of the room shirtless, her mouth parted sexily. She turns where she stands, and one stride at a time she makes her way to me.

She reaches out to touch me and I strike my hand out and fist her hair before she can make contact.

I bring her mouth a hair's length away from mine and really look at her. She whimpers in my hold, and I notice how dry her hair feels in my hand compared to Alessandra's silky brown locks. How her red lipstick looks cheap against Alessandra's pink lip gloss. I shove Gia away and growl at where my head is. I'm always horny, and love to fuck multiple times in a night. *What the hell is wrong with me?*

Heading to the chair, I lean back and close my eyes. Yeah, if I don't see Gia I won't compare the difference between her and Alessandra. I need to get my head straight, and having Gia's familiar touch will bring my head back to where it needs to be.

I feel her slide between my legs, and fumble with my jeans. My dick is still flaccid, not even slightly excited. *What the fuck?* Blowing out a ragged breath I look over and find a rolled blunt on the table. Don't mind if I do, I need it more than whoever left it.

I grab it and open the drawer in hopes of finding a lighter. I find a small blue one and giant purple dildo right next to it. Grabbing the lighter, I light the end of the blunt and take a deep breath. The green remedy fills my lungs, and relaxes my mind.

"You okay, baby?" Gia coos, her eyes fluttering with concern. I'm sure she cares about me on some fucked up level, but you can never be sure here. Girls want the alpha, the man wearing the cut so they can feel like they're special. If I told Gia to take a hike I wouldn't be surprised if she jumped on another brother's dick in a heartbeat. I can't trust her.

"Shut up," I hiss, taking a drag off the blunt.

She stands, and turns, pulling her skirt over her ass. Tan lines mark her round ass that reminds me of two globes. I love a big ass. Reaching out, I rub at one cheek roughly before slapping the skin as hard as I can. She winces as her hand slides down between her legs. She acts like she likes it rough, but I'm not so sure she does.

"You want to stick your dick in my ass?" she moans, her hair falling down her back. My dick jumps at that thought, but it's still not enough. Not close.

"Get Dolly," I order her. Maybe if I get two girls in here my dick will be pleased. She stands and looks at me with pouty lips. Gia's jealousy isn't cute on her. "Get her, or get the fuck out," I bark, not in the mood for her shit.

Gia steps to the door and hollers for Dolly, not bothering to push her skirt back down.

Seconds later Dolly walks in half drunk. Not surprising, ever since Zeek fell for Jillian, Dolly has been lost as to what to do next. Staggering in, I notice the top of her red dress is so loose her tits are flopping everywhere, her pink panties are showing from the bottom of the dress riding up. The bridge of her nose is broke, and her makeup is thick trying to cover the black eye Alessandra gave her. Dragging my bottom lip in-between my teeth I try to keep from smiling.

"Hey, baby," Dolly coos at me.

Rubbing the bridge of my nose, I can't find an ounce of horniness in me. Alessandra fucking broke me. The girls giggle, reminding me they're there. Being with Black Bird made me feel like I crossed a line I didn't belong on, but I can't for the life of me drag my ass to that bed and fuck these two girls. My dick just isn't into it. It had something much sweeter and finer, and refuses to go back to something old and worn.

Opening the drawer, I fist the giant dildo. "Fuck her in the ass," I instruct Dolly, before tossing her the fake dick. Gia's eyes light up excitedly, and Dolly rubs her hands along the rubber silicone like she just hit the fucking lottery.

It's hard to have respect for these women when they don't respect themselves.

Dolly kisses Gia playfully, and Gia kisses her back. Both of them keeping their eyes on me as they make out together. Gia's hands slide over Dolly's bare breast slowly her nipples budding from the touch. They fall onto the bed together, and Gia sticks her ass into the air ready for the purple eggplant to slam in her ass.

"Spit on this?" Dolly outstretches her hand, the dildo in it. I lift a brow, I'm not spitting on that thing.

Getting the hint, she shrugs and spits on it herself before turning back to Gia and shoving it in her ass slowly. Her ass opens up for it easily, and she moans like a porn star. Dolly pinches her own nipple as she slips the dick in as far as it will go. The sound of the rubber dick slamming into Gia's ass makes a slurping sound just before she moans out with pleasure.

Sitting back in my chair I blow a cloud of smoke as I watch the two. Tanned legs, fake tits, and tacky hair tangle in the bed before me. As I watch them, I'm trying to make sense of the woman in the other room.

Why her damaged past makes me want her more, to see past the fact she's a cop and I'm a traitor to my blood.

"Fuck me harder!" Gia moans, and Dolly's arm works faster

as she pumps it into her.

Tilting my head to the side I inhale the earthy tones and think maybe I'm thinking too hard.

If I want Alessandra, why not just fucking take her. My president claimed a sheriff, so am I really betraying my bloodline or are we evolving into a smarter breed.

Shaking my head, I'm not sure. The only thing that is standing in my way is her badge, and by the looks of Alessandra, she's no fucking cop.

I just need her to see that.

The girls climax together, moaning and howling sexily.

Stubbing the joint out in the palm of my hand, I stand. The girls falling on the bed out of breath, and the dildo in Dolly's hand. If Alessandra has taught me anything, it's that there is a difference between being a freak and a ho. These girls are the latter, and their act is getting stale.

"Where are you going?" Dolly asks out of breath, working her tired arm.

"Thanks for the show ladies," I mutter. I mean, I'm not a complete asshole, I'm going to thank them for their company. Even if I wasn't the one getting off.

That's a fucking first.

Entering my room, I slowly close the door, sliding along it until my ass hits the floor. It's dark, and the smell of forbidden sex lingers within the air.

Sitting from afar I watch Black Bird sleep naked in my bed. The blankets wrapped around her and her chocolate hair splayed on my pillow.

I hate her and want her. I want to kill her but feel every inch of her soft skin while I fuck her while she moans my name.

It's fucking confusing.

SIX
ALESSANDRA

Not being able to sleep, I slide off the bed and find a clean pair of panties, shorts, and pull a t-shirt off the floor over my head. Crossing my arms hiding my hard nipples, I look outside for Machete keeping watch on me. There's nobody, and the hallway is dark. Slipping out I quickly shut the door, so Rocky can't get out and tiptoe down the hall. The sound of moaning coming from a room in passing. Sounds… interesting.

Coming to the bar, I step behind it and grab a bottle of tequila and a shot glass. The floor is sticky and grimy beneath my feet, and it smells like cigarettes and perfume.

"Make that two?"

I jump in panic, falling into the line of liquor sitting on the shelf behind me. Jillian sits on a barstool at the end of the bar concealed in the dark. The only light coming from a couple of neon signs hanging on the wall around us.

"You scared the shit out of me!" I huff, and she smiles.

"Sorry, Zeek woke me up for sex and now I can't sleep," she informs matter of fact. "But from the sound of it, I think both of us got lucky," she winks, and I quickly look down at the bar for that second shot glass. I don't know what Felix and I did, or what it means. I don't want to think about it either. "Oh, I see. Not going to give me the details?"

"There's nothing to tell," I reply sharply.

"Mhhm," she responds cheekily. Pouring her a glass I slide it over to her and she catches it.

"Just shut up and drink," I sass, pouring my own shot. Downing my shot it burns all the way down, and I'm hoping it works fast as I want the voices in my head to shut up.

"I'm just saying if you did... I get it. These men are a force you can't deny. Trust me." She shakes her head, sliding the glass back over to me.

"I'm just doing some business with him," I tell her and this piques her interest, anything to get her off the whole sex thing. She won't get it because I don't get it.

"My dad... wasn't really my dad apparently." Jillian gasps, covering her mouth. "I am just trying to get some answers about him, who he was, how he died. All of it," I tell her, my eyes focused on the granite bar as I ramble what is on my mind.

"I am at a loss for words," she mutters.

"Makes two of us," I reply, pouring another glass and pounding it back. Leaning across the bar, I stare at my best friend, someone I trust more than anyone in the world. "But I think finding out the truth is going to do more than I think," I tell her, my eyes glossing over.

"What do you mean?" she tilts her head to the side. Sighing, I dig my nail into a chip on the bar.

"I don't know," I mumble. "Being here I feel... like a side of me I never knew existed is being pulled from the grave if that makes sense." I raise a brow at her and she looks at me confused.

"Forget it," I shake my head trying to muster a smile. "I'm

just tired and over-thinking things."

"Well, fucking an outlaw will do that to ya," Jillian retorts. Rolling my eyes I slide out from behind the bar and flip her off.

"Goodnight," I state.

"Hey Alessandra, is he a cock-a-saurous Rex?" she winks, taunting me. Her and I used to laugh back in the day about Zeek having a dick the size of a Rex, so of course she would flip it around on me.

Walking back to my room I can't help but laugh and yell, "Bigger!"

It true, it's taking everything I have not to waddle when I walk, he fucked me so good.

Climbing back into bed, I stare at the wall nibbling at my bottom lip. It was a one-night stand, a moment of weakness obviously. The bedroom door opens and shuts, the familiar smell of Felix filling the room. I close my eyes and pretend to be asleep, hoping the bed dips and he lies next to me. Seconds that feel like minutes pass and I don't hear or feel anything so I slowly look over my shoulder finding Felix sitting on the floor with his head leaned back against the door.

He looks tormented, but sexy. It's got to be that sexy man bun and beard that bring me to my knees. He's so rugged, and rough looking I crave his rough touch.

He stirs and I quickly roll back over, making sure to moan and hike the blanket up my thigh a little. What can I say? I'm a tease.

Rolling over I glance at the door where I last saw Felix last night. He had his head leaned back and was sleeping against the door. It was like watching a lion at rest. He seemed peaceful, but intimidating at the same time. Rubbing at my collarbone I wonder what the events of last night mean, if they mean anything. Rubbing my thighs together I feel sore, beautifully sore.

I am used to having random hook-ups, but last night there was something different about it.

Like there was so much hate and tension built up that you couldn't help the heat bonding us together.

What am I saying, Felix will never be with a cop.

Sighing, I slide out of bed and shuffle through my bag for some clean clothes. I'll change into my uniform at the department, as I don't want to get the club riled up wearing it here. Standing up straight I suddenly notice Rocky isn't in here. I wonder if Felix took him when he woke up. I hope he's with someone responsible.

Walking into the bathroom I notice the counter is spotless as everything was randomly tossed on the floor from the throes of last night. Images of Felix and me together flash behind my eyes and my nipples suddenly ache from the reminder. Shaking my head of the memories, I tip my head over and pile my brown hair into a messy bun as I don't want to fish the hairbrush out of the trashcan. Raising my head, I notice the mirror is split from our tryst, showing two sides of me and I don't think it's a coincidence. I feel different being around the criminals, and maybe that's why Felix's statement about not being so different hit me so hard.

Like my urge to snap someone's neck when they've hurt a child instead of take them into custody. The way I don't see drugs as being terrible and experiment myself. These are parts of me I don't understand and feel that aren't normal. I've known that my whole life, but have refused to acknowledge the difference between me and others. My urge to sin, have fun, and live wild are becoming hard to ignore being around the side that lives free and by their own laws.

Stepping outside the room, Dolly and Gia come out of a room across from me. Their clothes are disheveled, and their makeup is running down their face like Popsicles left out in the sun too long.

"My ass is so sore from fucking Felix," Gia whines, and my heart falls from my chest hearing her say that.

"That's nothing, I saw Machete fuck someone with the handle of his ax last week," Dolly laughs and cringes. I bite my inner cheek as I click the door shut behind me, thus gaining their attention.

"Oh, we didn't see you there," Dolly plays innocent. I give a tight-lipped smile, acting as if I'm indifferent to whatever they're getting at.

Continuing my way down the hall Gia grabs my forearm, her grip tight. My eyes slowly fall to her hand, and I can't help but notice it reeks of rancid pussy.

"Don't get any ideas about Felix, he's claimed, honey. Besides, no cop has any business here," she sneers.

"You were just the thrill of the chase, sweetheart," Dolly states.

"An easy chase at that," Gia laughs, letting me go.

My breathing picks up as I feel like I'm in high school all over again. Glaring at Dolly, I eye her dark eyes from where I elbowed her the other day.

"Nice eye shadow," I insult, and her nostrils flare with hostility. Head held high I continue my way through the club, fighting back tears. I don't know why I feel so hurt, I didn't have sex with Felix expecting anything. Yet, this weight on my chest is crushing.

On the couch sits Machete and Rocky. Machete is feeding

him jerky and ruffling up his puppy hair around his face. Rocky seems happy, as Machete does too.

"There you are," I half laugh, half choke on emotion.

"Oh yeah. He was scratching to get out this morning, so I let him out. I hope that's okay?" Machete informs.

I nod. "Yes of course. Thank you." Only a crazy person would disagree with him, especially hearing what he did with the handle of his ax.

"Hey baby, you look like you could use some coffee this morning?" Carola suggests from behind the bar.

"Coffee? You have coffee?" I ask with more gusto than I intended. She laughs and turns around grabbing a mug.

"How else do you think I get through the day with these boys? Then again, I do add whiskey to mine." She laughs to herself, before planting a mug of hot coffee on the counter.

Cupping it with both hands, I take a sip. It's black, which isn't usually my go-to, and it's hot. I like iced coffee, with lots of sugar but I wouldn't ever turn down a cup of joe. Coffee is a liquid hug.

"Hey, you working today?" The familiar voice of Felix tears down my spine like the claws of a cat. Placing the cup down, I turn on my heel, avoiding eye contact.

"Yeah, I can take myself," I inform. The way he fucked me like he couldn't get enough, and then couldn't get away fast enough isn't lost on me. I feel used, and hate how attracted I am to him.

"How are you going to do that, your car is at your place. Remember?" He tilts his head to the side, trying to look me in the eye.

"I'll walk or something," I mutter pushing passed him.

Outside the weather is cloudy but warm, the smell of rain is thick in the air.

"What the fuck is your problem?" Felix barks from behind me. I scoff, is he serious?

"I don't have a problem, I just think we need to stay away from each other is all," I insist, not bothering to stop and talk to him. We're just a sweet disaster waiting to happen.

He wraps an arm around my waist, stopping me in my tracks.

"Whoa! What's with the fucking tone?" his brows furrow.

"Don't give me that shit!" I snap, and his eyes widen like I slapped him. "I'm not stupid, I know what last night was, and I'm a big girl I can handle it. What I don't appreciate is you fucking me, and then literally going and fucking the club whore right after!" I point at the club's door and his jaw ticks, his shoulders tensing beneath his cut.

"I'm sorry, was there fine print somewhere that said once I fuck you? That I'm to be monogamous to a cop?"

Heat flaring to unbearable lengths my hand slips from my waist and lands right across his face.

His head whips to the side and catcalls sound from the clubhouse.

"I'm just the cop, remember? So stay the fuck away from me!" My throat clogs with emotion, tears wanting to spill their heart out. I can't believe I let him get to me.

"What the fuck is going on out here?" Zeek roars, stepping out of the clubhouse. His eyes land on me and Felix and I look away.

"I need a ride to work," I mutter, not addressing the situation between Felix and I. Zeek looks between Felix and I catching on to the tension between us.

"Bomber Jack will take you in the SUV," Zeek clips dryly. His eyes boring into Felix like he wants to strangle him. For what, I don't know but I want to do the same right now. Maybe because Felix wasn't supposed to sleep with me, or maybe he hid his attraction toward me from his president.

"Great," I whisper softly making sure to avoid eye contact with Felix.

Sliding into the leather passenger seat I can't help but glance back at Felix in the mirror. Zeek is yelling at him and pointing at the clubhouse. He must have done something pretty bad, as I've never seen Zeek yell at him before. Felix's face is red, his hair blowing in the wind as his eyes focus on the SUV like he can see me staring at him.

Leaning my head back on the headrest, Bomber Jack climbs in talking about something, but my head is somewhere else to really listen. I need more coffee. I need away from the outlaws actually.

Looks like Felix and I are back to where we were.

Hating one another.

Like it's supposed to be.

Cop and outlaw.

FELIX

"What the fuck? Tell me what I think happened, didn't happen!" Zeek barks at me like a disobedient child. It pisses me off. Puffing my shoulders out I get right in his face. He's my president, but he's also my fucking cousin. My blood. I think he forgets we grew up together.

"What?" he juts his chin, silently challenging me. Everyone is surrounding us, hoping we break out in a fight. If I didn't have so much respect for him, I'd fight his ass right here.

"Who I stick my dick in doesn't concern you," I spit back, turning away I head to my bike.

Zeek steps in my way, his boots scuffing against the concrete.

"It does when it's in my clubhouse. It does when it concerns my ol' lady." He points to himself. Jillian will be more than furious if I hurt Alessandra, and will bitch to Zeek. "But most of all what about all the shit you gave me about fucking a sheriff!"

My brows furrow, remorse not settling well within my bones. I did give him shit, and I still will.

"You don't think I feel like a disloyal bastard screwing around with her? Huh?" I shout, my brows furrowing as my gut knots from the betrayal setting heavy on me.

Zeek shoves me, and I shove him back just as he throws my hands off of him. Nose to nose, I can feel the heat radiating off him, the eyes staring at us to see who will throw a punch.

Truth is I can't make this right, I fucked Alessandra and knew when I did I was handing over more than my dick.

"She's more than a fucking cop, she just doesn't know it yet," I counter, my own words surprising me.

"Yeah, I get that but why haven't you told her?"

I shake my head, rubbing the hair lining my chin. I can't tell her. I feel like she needs to find out who she is before I give her the answer. I've seen what Alessandra is capable of by a glimpse of her past. She's lost and I'm the reaper that's willing to show her the dark side. The tips of her white angelic wings are dipped in black, she just needs to be held under to fully commit to her inner demons.

Zeek growls, slamming his fist into the side of the shed next to where we park our bikes.

"This won't end well, brother," he replies softly. "She has baggage," he mutters and my head snaps in his direction.

"This is your fucking fault to begin with. If you wouldn't have made me a goddamn babysitter and stuck to the bylaws of an outlaw, I wouldn't have gotten close to Alessandra and seen her for something more than a snitch. But you did, and now I'm all fucked up!" I roar, pointing to my head. The shit in my head is not well. The urge to hurt Alessandra and care for her all in one, not normal. To feel her delicate skin, then tear into her like I hate her. It's an impulse I have to control every time I'm near her.

Looking down I sigh.

Suddenly Gia appears smoking a cigarette outside with a Red Bull in her hand. Pushing past Zeek I stomp toward her. Pissed she went and told Alessandra I fucked her, done with her fucking claiming ass.

Coming up to her I knock the Red Bull right out of her hand, and her eyes snap to mine in panic.

"What the fuck?" she snaps angrily.

Slamming my hands into the wall, a hand on each side of her head I get right in her face.

"Stay away from Alessandra or your ass is gone, do you understand me?" I sneer, and her eyes widen.

"But—"

"We're done," I ground out between clenched teeth, taking a step back I eye her like the slut that she is and shake my head.

I need to find Alessandra and set shit straight. She will listen, or I will fucking make her.

SEVEN

ALESSANDRA

Sitting in my cruiser, I take a sip of my iced coffee loaded with sugar. *Man, I needed this.* Coffee is like rocket fuel for a cop.

Looking up, a young man about the age of fifteen stands on the corner just ahead. Furrowing my brows I watch him closely. This being an alley, I wasn't expecting to see anyone back here as I took my coffee break. A black Neon pulls up to him, and the young man leans into the window handing the driver something before the car drives off.

Shit. He's dealing drugs.

Putting my coffee down, I pull around the corner and flip my lights on. The kid's eyes flash with panic before he throws his arms out in disbelief he'd been caught.

Getting out of my car, I keep my hand on my gun. These kids are unpredictable when it comes to slinging drugs. Their bosses will have their fingers if they don't return with money or drugs, leaving the kids desperate.

"What are you doing out here?" I ask in a friendly but stern tone.

He raises a brow, not speaking a word because we both

know what he's doing out here.

Stepping up to him he's almost as tall as I am. He's handsome for his age. Short brown hair, sharp jaw, and piercing blue eyes. He looks like he's had it rough just by looking in his eyes let alone his clothes. His black shirt looks dirty though, and his jeans are worn out.

"What's your name?" I question.

He looks down, still not wanting to speak to me.

"Look, if you want to do this the hard way that's fine," I scoff, reaching for my cuffs. I can be just like every other straight cop if that's how he wants to play it.

"Bishop," he grumbles, and I stall, my hand falling from my cuffs. Eyeing him, I wonder what drugs he's selling. Simple weed, or something worse.

"Turn around." I twirl my finger wanting him to face the cruiser. Sighing heavily, he plants two palms on the hood of the car, obviously knowing the drill.

I pat him down, finding a baggie of weed, and crack in his back pocket. *Jesus Christ. He's a fucking kid.* It angers me to see these drug lords finding such young kids and giving them such powerful drugs to deal.

"Why are you out here dealing this crap?" I ask, tossing the shit on the hood.

He sneers as if I'm an idiot.

"You wouldn't know shit about living out here," he spits back.

"So why don't you tell me then, make me see it." I cross my arms, intrigued to hear his story. I know it won't be pretty, and that is why I take compassion on cases like this. Because I do understand. I've seen mothers stealing milk from grocery stores just to feed their children. I've seen kids running drugs because they got kicked out of school. The streets are hard, and I want to help.

"My mom is sick, and nobody will hire me because of where I live. I'm doing what I have to, to take care of my family," he informs with more confidence than a lot of people I find dealing dope do. They either blame it on a friend, or it's not theirs. Something stupid.

"Your loyalty is admirable," I mutter. He shakes his head, not saying anything. I can tell he's the strong, quiet type.

"Who do you work for?" I interrogate, hoping he will tell me so I can bust the fuck who is hiring out kids. He doesn't speak a word though.

Feeling my back pocket for cash I pull out two-hundred bucks, I can't remember why it's there, probably forgot to pay a bill, and toss it in front of him.

"Tell whomever you work for you're done," I demand.

Bishop turns around, eyeing me like I've lost my mind. "My boss ain't just going to let me go," he laughs condescendingly.

"You work for the Sin City Outlaws now," I continue and the boy's throat bobs as he swallows hard. He knows as well as I do nobody will question the Outlaws. "You're done with this shit. You are going to head over to their club and tell them... Jillian sent you." Nobody will care if I sent him, but they will if Queen Jillian did. "They will put you to work, and protect you if you have what it takes," I offer, totally throwing Jillian under the bus. Drug lords out here don't give a shit about these kids. If Bishop runs into trouble, they will turn their back or kill them. He's lived his life in the throes of the streets, so there is no rehabilitating him.

Bishop lowers his head, rubbing at his cheeks as he mulls it over.

"It's that, or I take you in," I clip.

His blue eyes shoot to mine, a tick in his hard jaw. He

knows as well as I do that if whoever he works for catches wind of him being taken in by the cops, he's in trouble. I don't want to put him in harm's way, that is why I'm doing this in the first place.

"Okay, I'll do it," he swipes the cash from the hood with force.

"Good." I give a curt nod. "Head over there now then."

Bishop walks away, looking over his shoulder at me before turning the corner.

I could have taken him in, but he would just be back out here slinging drugs tonight. He'd be shot or killed before he was twenty-one. At least with the Outlaws, he will have a better chance at surviving the streets because he's shit at dealing drugs. I spotted him easily.

Grabbing the drugs off the hood of my car, I sling them into the gutter of the street. The rainwater taking them down the sewer. Sliding into my cruiser, I look at the MDT to make sure I didn't miss a call. I'm supposed to pick Raven up here soon, she had a family meeting and is starting her shift late.

Looking down the street, I watch trash tumble across the grimy street, the blazing sun causing a haze to waft from the pavement. It's not the prettiest scenery, but it's typically quiet back here.

A knock on my window has me scream and nearly spill my coffee. It's fucking Felix.

Rolling my window down I have the sudden urge to tase him for scaring the shit out of me.

"What the fuck are you doing here? How did you find me?" I ramble off a series of questions.

"I can always find you, Black Bird," he replies huskily. His words coming out with promise and making my toes curl in my boots. "Your suspect is getting away," he mouths, pointing in the direction of where Bishop just turned.

Pursing my lips, I look away. Fuck, I've been caught being a bad cop. Again.

He leans down resting his arms on the window seal. "We need to talk," he demands.

I shake my head. "No, we don't. I told you to leave me alone."

He laughs. "Yeah, you don't make the rules, sweetheart, I do. Besides, you think I'm an asshole, and I'm not an asshole, you're just being a bitch."

Jerking my door open, I climb out and shove Felix with all my might. Having enough of him and his damn controlling ways.

"What the hell is your problem!" I shove him again, knocking him back a few steps. He flicks his chin with his fingers, a smirk pulling at his lips. Lips I remember tasting and biting last night. He's amused by my temper, go figure.

Reaching out to shove him one last time, he lashes out and takes my wrist into his hard grasp. He jerks me to get my attention, and my eyes flutter with the amount of control he has. Reminding me how strong, and virile he really is.

"You. You are my fucking problem!" he seethes in my face. His dark eyes holding me where I stand. I relax in his hold and take a ragged breath. I hate how I want him and don't, all at the same time. It's tiring, and I can't tell if I want to run or climb him like a tree.

He steps forward, pushing me backward. "Can we talk?" he says calmly, his wild eyes looking me up and down.

I don't respond as I clench my teeth. I hear the door to my cruiser open, and I'm shoved into the back seat. The hard plastic biting into my back. He climbs over me, shutting the door behind him.

"You don't want to fucking talk? Fine, how about we just let our bodies figure this shit out then, huh?" He tilts his head to the side as his fingers fling off my utility belt. My body comes alive, but my pride defies the warmth building in my chest.

"I'm still a cop," I remind him.

"Shut up," he snaps, his hands sliding up my arms and pinning them above my head, his lips brushing against my skin and my eyes roll into the back of my head. He's right, our bodies have a language of their own.

Sexual impulse races through my veins and I can't help but pull from his grip and grab him by the back of the neck, pulling his mouth to mine. Needing him closer to me, to touch him, and taste him.

He chased me down. He's here with me. That stands for something, right?

I've never had a man go to great lengths to get my attention before.

Placing my feet on the door, I lift my ass off the seat as he shimmies my pants and panties down to my knees. The warmth of him in-between my legs blazes to my core making my clit tick in excitement. Unzipping his jeans, I see the outline of his length and my heart begins to flutter with the anticipation of his cock filling me, stretching me into bliss.

Shoving his hand down his pants he pulls it out, and it's hard and long with a bead of excitement about to drip from the tip. Leaning forward I flick my tongue at it and his hand slips into my hair softly.

"Take me in your mouth," he whispers. Keeping my eyes on him, I open my mouth and he slides it in. The ridge of the tip skimming along my teeth slightly as it hits the back of my throat. Hollowing out my cheeks I suck with all my might, and he hisses with satisfaction as his head lolls back.

"Oh fuck, right there," he grounds out between clenched teeth.

I bob my head back and forth, his cock pulsing in my mouth every time my lips come in contact with the tip. He is salty and sweet all at the same time.

Letting go of my hair he presses on my chest, pushing me back down onto the seat

He raises my legs, my pants around my ankles and raises them over his head, my legs wrapped around his strong torso. Keeping him close.

The windows begin to fog with our heavy breathing, the radio in the front going off about a robbery in progress. I don't fucking care though, all I can think about is Felix on top of me. Inside of me.

Using a single finger, he slides it between my legs and through my wetness. My hips buck on their own accord a moan spilling from my lips.

"I love that sound," he whispers, positioning himself between my thighs.

The tip hits my heat, and then with one quick jerk he's inside of me. Bare.

I feel all of him. The veins, the tip, the ridge. My toes curl in my boots, my eyes rolling in the back of my head as I push my hips up to gain more friction.

The car rocks as he drives into me over and over again, each thrust taking me higher into the field of pleasure. The way he feels on top of me brings a sense of security and comfort. The heat of his body soaking into mine, our bodies tangled into one. It's as if we can't get enough of each other. What we have is forbidden by the public's eye, but how can it when it feels this good between my legs? His teeth nip at my earlobe, and his hand cradles my neck. This right here, him holding my neck does something to me I will never be able to explain.

The sound of voices outside the cruiser cause me to hold my breath in panic, and Felix's eyes shoot up. Using his hand, he cups my mouth, keeping an eye on the people just outside the window.

Slowly, he continues to fuck me. The excitement we might get caught, the forbiddenness of us being together heightening my arousal that much more.

"Oh fuck, the cops are on our block. We better warn the rest." A deep voice sounds from just outside the window.

"Fucking pigs!" A kick sounds at the front of the car, as if someone just kicked it.

The voices become lighter as they drift further down the block. Felix keeps his eye on the window, but I can't take my eyes off of him as he continues to fuck me.

As if he can sense me staring at him he looks down at me, his long hair falling in his face.

A smile pulls at his hard lips and pressure builds in my core where I begin to move with him. His brows narrow as he picks up the pace, the car begins to rock and I tense as a rush of bliss makes me feel so high I don't want to come down.

I release everything in my being, giving it over to Felix. He tenses, his body jerking as warmth fills my pussy.

We still, trying to catch our breath. Staring into one another's eyes.

I tuck a piece of his hair behind his ear, my stomach in knots with what I'm about to ask but I can't keep up with his games.

"What are we doing here, Felix?"

He sighs heavily and rubs my cheek softly.

"I don't know," he whispers honestly. "I won't love you. I'm not capable of the emotion," he admits.

Tilting my cramped neck to the side, I narrow my brows. "Well, I won't love you back," I laugh, and he smiles. God when he smiles, which isn't often, it's as if someone literally just ripped my heart from my chest. It's so rugged, lazy, yet incredibly handsome. Just like a biker should smile.

"I can't make up my mind what I want when it comes to you. You… scare me," he whispers, tucking a hair behind his ear. Squinting my eyes, I squirm under him because I too am scared of him. He makes me feel things that aren't normal, nothing about us being together is normal.

"I should be going, I have to pick up Raven," I tell him.

He nods. "Be back at the clubhouse tonight," he demands, rather than asks. I want to confide my insecurities of being at the club. Tell him how much I want to claw Gia and Dolly's eyes out, but I know first hand how un-sexy that is. I need to stand my ground when it comes to those two hooches.

I fidget under him, everything about this morning returning. Gia and Dolly.

"I didn't fuck them," he confides, and my eyes shoot to his. It's as if he read my mind. "I'm many things but I wouldn't do that to you."

"I don't care," I shrug, looking to the side.

"Right," he scoffs, before sitting up. "I guess you storming out this morning is how you normally act after getting fucked to the point you forget how to breathe?" He shoots me a look and I swallow hard. He has me there, I was pissed and wanted out of there this morning and wouldn't normally act that way after a night of unforgettable sex.

"What did you expect when I was bombarded with women who can give you things I can't?" I avoid eye contact as I just revealed my insecurities.

“Who says you can’t?” he replies ruggedly. Ignoring him I reach down to pull my pants up and then it hits me. We are in the back seat. The doors lock from the inside.

“Um, Felix? How are we going to get out?”

He looks around. “Shit, I forgot about that,” he states irritated. He tries to roll the window down, but it doesn’t work. He grabs the faceplate on the door handle and jerks it off in one pull, breaking it. He really is like Tarzan.

“What are you doing?” I gasp in horror. He grabs at the wires, piecing them together, and then tries the window again. It rolls down. My mouth drops in astonishment.

Reaching out the window he opens the door from the outside and climbs out. Meanwhile, I’m still sitting here looking at the door like an idiot. How did he know how to do that? Wait, who am I kidding. He’s a fucking criminal, and the way he fucks me so good, I often forget that. I slide out of the backseat and go about fixing my hair as he rolls the window back up and tries to put the faceplate back the way it was. But it’s broken, there is no fixing it.

“I’ll figure something out. I’ll arrest someone and blame it on them or something,” I tell him.

He chuckles, shutting the door. Grabbing me by the shirt he pulls me to him and bites at my lips, but I pull away before he can make contact. God, I just want to lay in that back seat with him all day.

“Go get the bad guys.” He stops, looking at the sky with an odd look. “Or let them go, I’m not really sure what it is you do.” He tilts his head to the side and I flip him off. He has no idea what it’s like to have to judge every person that walks my way.

“I only arrest the ones who deserve it. That boy is just in a tough situation; he didn’t deserve to have his life ruined when I had the potential to possibly change it for the better.” I shrug.

Felix's whole face softens, as he looks at me with an unreadable look.

"What?"

He shakes his head, turning away. Giving a second look, he glances at me with dark eyes before making his way to his bike. There was something unspoken there, I just don't know what it was.

Why does this have to be so hard?

"How'd the family meeting go? Everything okay?" I ask Raven as she slides into the cruiser. Her hair is messy, and her uniform is wrinkled. She smells like dirt, and her eyes have dark circles under them like she'd been crying.

She looks at me with a confused look before snapping to. "Oh! Yeah, it will be," she fake smiles, buckling up. I smile, not really sure what she's talking about. Then again, Raven is an odd girl.

Raising my hand to flip her visor up, Raven flinches and slaps at me out of fear. My eyes widen, as she looks at me with pinched brows.

"I'm sorry. I..."

"No, it's okay," I assure her, but my curiosity has me wondering why she just acted like a battered wife when I raised my hand.

"I just need some coffee or something. Didn't get much sleep," she mutters, looking out the window with red cheeks.

"I can always do coffee," I mask a smile and head toward my favorite coffee shop.

"So how have you been?" Raven asks as we sit outside the coffee shop. I shrug, eyeing the MDT with my coffee in hand. I can smell Felix on me, smell our scent lingering from the back seat.

"Fine, I guess." I try and mask my after sex glow, my walking on cloud fucking nine excitement.

She scoffs. "Yeah right. I can tell something is going on. Is it something with Jillian or the club?"

I lift an eye at her and her intrusive questioning. I wonder if she saw me with Felix or another member. Wouldn't surprise me the way The Sin City Outlaws are always following me around.

"There is a 403, at Rangeline," I change the subject.

"Oh a prowler!" Raven says with excitement. I flinch that she actually knows that code, she never knows them. Looks like someone did their homework. Or got lucky.

"Yes… it is," I say, eyeing her from the side.

I blow out a breath and turn the sirens on, heading in the way of the chaos and mischief.

Pulling up to the residence it's a small one-story house in a neighborhood that doesn't normally get a lot of violence. The house looks empty, as there's no blinds or curtains in the windows. There are flowerbeds out front, and a birdbath right in the center. A stone walkway leads to the front door - which is open.

"731, we are on scene of the 403," I inform dispatch.

"Copy that. 14:15," dispatch replies back with the time.

Getting out of the car, I pull my gun from my holster and look around the parameter. Raven steps in front of me, obviously wanting to take charge. I let her, as she really needs the experience.

She steps into the house, making sure to look both ways

with her gun raised.

"Las Vegas Police!" I announce, but it's silent.

Raven steps into the other room, before coming out of a door behind me.

"It's clear," she huffs out of breath. Lowering my gun, I narrow my brows at the scene, or lack thereof.

"The front door is open, but nothing is taken or disturbed," I inform, stepping into the kitchen.

Just then a sharp, hot pain radiates through my lower abdomen. Lowering my head to the pain, I notice a black-gloved hand pull a small knife out of my stomach. Blood spills behind the blade, staining my uniform and dripping on the cracked tile. My lips tremble as I follow the hand to an arm of a masked man or woman. Blood drips so fast from the cut, I become woozy instantly. I fall to the floor, clutching my side to try and stop the bleeding. The intruder leans down, and I grab for my gun. He snatches my radio and kicks me over before I can even get my gun out.

"Fuck!" I cry, furious and angry.

Raven's department issued boots come into my line of sight as she casually walks into the kitchen, and I gasp in pain. Glancing up at her, her eyes fall to mine, and she just stares at me.

"Go get him," I heave but she just looks at me in silence. "Did you stop him?" I ask, but she's stoic, just staring at me with narrowed brows. "Raven! Get help, do something!" I cry, the pain too much to bear.

Sirens sound from outside, and Raven's head snaps in that direction.

"Sheriff's department!" is hollered from the living room.

"In here!" I cry. Raven suddenly falls to her knees and covers my wound with her hands.

"Oh my God, what happened?" she asks in a tone of surprise. I eye her like she's lost her mind. Did she black out or something? What the hell is going on?

A man jogs into the kitchen and finds us.

"Oh shit," he gasps. Grabbing the radio on his shoulder he calls it in, and an ambulance.

"I'm Chewie, and help is on the way. Is there anyone I can call?" he asks, looking oddly familiar. I think about calling Jillian, but that isn't smart. She needs to stay hidden being the president's ol' lady.

"What about Jillian?" Raven suggests like she read my mind.

I grab Raven's hand with my bloody one, my body trembling as warm blood pools under me.

"Do not call Jillian. Don't! She will freak out and come to the hospital," I tell her. Her eyes flash, but she doesn't say anything.

"Promise me, goddamn it!" I demand, needing her to understand, but she just continues to nod her head.

Seconds later an EMT is kneeling beside me, observing the slice in my side and pumping an IV of pain reliever into the crook of my arm.

Everything is a little fuzzy from the kitchen floor to being transported into the ambulance. My vision blurred and blacking around the edges.

I'm jostled back and forth as the ambulance bounces out of the driveway and onto the main road.

The medicine begins to relax me, and my mind wanders like a ping-pong ball in one of those games I played when I was younger. How did Raven miss that suspect in the kitchen? Will I die?

When did the suspect run off? I wonder if Rocky is okay at the club.

No, she gave an oath to protect me, her family in blue.

The sound of thunder vibrates the ambulance, and my skin prickles with the recognition. Using all my might I use my elbows to sit up and look out the windows of the ambulance finding Felix following us on his motorcycle, and a couple other club members. My chest fills with warmth that he's here, but I'm also pissed because that means Raven fucking called Jillian after I told her not to.

"Ma'am, please lay back down," the EMT insists, as he begins to attempt to patch my wound.

Lying back down, I can't help the big grin on my face. Giddiness racing through me like a young girl with a teenage crush. I may be sliced like a fucking fish right now, but Felix and the Outlaws are escorting *me* to the hospital making sure nothing else happens to me. I feel like family being protected, someone important.

A frown crosses my face, and I can't decide if I'm over thinking things or it's the medicine in my arm but which family do I belong to?

Law enforcement or The Outlaws?

FELIX

Riding next to the ambulance my heart beats in my chest faster than I can last remember. Jillian got a call from Alessandra's phone informing her there had been an accident, and she needed to come right away. It took everything Zeek had to make her stay at the clubhouse.

I stay right behind the bus making sure nobody else gets close to it. I don't know what happened, but I swear to God if it has anything to do with the club there will be repercussions.

My hand grips the throttle tightly as I hope Alessandra's okay. I should have been watching her at work too, I never should have left. Zeek put me in charge of protecting her, and I feel like I failed. This could be work related, but it might not be.

If anyone saw us together, any of our rivals could have taken my discretions out on her. Our club may dabble in law enforcement, but a lot of others find it as betraying the codes of an MC.

The ambulance pulls into the hospital and I park right on the sidewalk not giving a shit about the parking laws, my boys Machete, Gatz, and Mac are right behind me. I jog up to the bus just as they begin to wheel her out. Blood stains her uniform, and a large patch is placed on the side of her beautiful stomach.

My hands itch to fucking tear someone's head off for this. It looks painful, and the darkness inside of me wants to cause the terror that Alessandra might be feeling.

She's drugged up and seems happy to see me with that goofy ass grin on her face. All I can feel is the urge for revenge.

"What the fuck happened, Black Bird," I whisper, gripping her cold hand. She interlocks her tiny fingers in mine, her blood staining my skin. She doesn't reply, as an oxygen mask is slipped over her face.

"Sir, are you family?" The EMT with long blonde hair asks me skeptically. I didn't even notice she was there I was so involved with Alessandra. I look back down at Alessandra who stares at me longingly. She may be drugged, but I can see deep inside of those irises she's hurt and scared.

"Fuck yes, I'm family," I state forcefully, not taking my eyes off of her. I'm not letting her out of my sight, not until I know if this is club related or not. Not until I know she is okay.

"Well, okay then. Follow me." The EMT laughs, pushing the stretcher into the entrance of the hospital.

Looking over my shoulder to my boys I curl my hands into fists. "Someone will pay for this," I grit through clenched teeth.

Staring at Alessandra, she's fast asleep and on the path to recovery. The cut was deep but it was a clean cut, nothing major was hit. She had a blood transfusion and a shit ton of stitches though. Bomber Jack is just outside the door keeping watch, but I'm still wound tight as it seems nobody saw anything when this happened. Her partner said she didn't see anything. Shit like this doesn't go without repercussion, not in my world, and it's killing me to sit here idle. I'm bloodthirsty, and feeling like the fucking criminal I've been pegged for my whole life.

The hospital door opens, and I jump alert, my hand reaching for my gun. It's Zeek, with two cups in each of his hands.

I relax, sitting back in the stiff as hell recliner beside Alessandra.

"How is she?" Zeek asks, looking her over.

"She's good," I mutter, running my palm down my face. I'm fucking exhausted.

Zeek hands me a cup of coffee, and I take a small sip. It's good, but I really want a bottle of Jack right now. My mind is everywhere, and my fucking emotions are even worse.

Zeek leans against the wall, a raised brow in my direction. "Jillian is up my ass wanting to know what happened."

I sigh. "From what I got from her, her partner Raven checked the house and said it was clear and it obviously wasn't," I scoff. Nobody saw anything, or they ain't talking.

"The partner must have been the one who called Jillian. Has she shown up here?" Zeek questions.

"Not that I know of." I shake my head, setting the coffee down between my feet. Looking up at Zeek I clasp my hands together. "You don't think it was club related do you?"

Adjusting his stance, he blows out a steady breath. "Hard to tell at this point, we are all fucking targets. We need more information from her when she wakes up to tell for sure," he shrugs a shoulder.

"Well, when she wakes, I'm taking her back to the club. This place is a joke, she still has blood all over her," I huff, pointing at her side that is stained with dry blood.

Alessandra stirs, her hand flexing-looking for mine. Quickly I lace my fingers with hers, letting her know that I'm here and she settles.

She's pushing her way into my fucked up way of life. With her smart mouth, dark past, and sexy legs. I didn't have a chance to begin with. She may look innocent and sweet, but she knows how to leave her mark on a man.

"Have you told her yet?"

"About what?" My tone vague, I know what he's talking about but I'm not ready to tell her that. She has a past, and has a monster deep inside of her. I'm just not sure how dark that monster is once it's been released.

"You know what," Zeek snaps.

Inhaling a deep breath, I shake my head.

"Not yet," I mutter.

"Just... Just, make sure you know what you're doing brother," Zeek's voice is soft, but his point is sharp. His eyes on mine and Alessandra's tangled fingers. I don't like the way his stare makes me feel.

I shoot my eyes to his, anger pumping my chest.

"What does that mean?" I snap, wanting so bad to take Alessandra away from everyone so we can just be us and alone. Not having to worry about labels or what people think, what we think. Just us, doing what we fucking do best.

"Means… I've never seen you like this." Both of his brows raise to his hairline, his tone laced with surprise, maybe even a hint of fear.

Glancing back at Alessandra the look of her hits me in the chest. That unfamiliar feeling taking hold of me again. It's a mixture of feelings that don't even belong in the same sentence let alone to feel all at the same time. Lust, fear, dominant, protector, jealousy, vengeful, love.

"That makes two of us brother," I whisper.

I've never had someone care about me, or to teach me how to love someone outside the club.

I'm not normally scared of new things, it comes with the territory of an outlaw. But this, I'm fucking terrified because I don't think I can give Alessandra what she deserves.

A man that is capable of normal emotions. I'm biker trash, and that's all I'll ever be able to give her. A world of chaos and demons.

Waking up I feel stiff and very sore, and my hand is sweaty and cramped. Opening my eyes, I follow my arm down to my hand finding Felix asleep in the chair holding it.

As if he can sense me awake, his eyes snap open, and he sits up straight.

"How are you feeling?" he asks huskily, rubbing his face with his free hand.

"Like someone stabbed me," I croak. I shift in the hard bed, not very comfortable and I'm starving for something greasy.

"I want to get you out of here, take you back to the club," Felix states, wasting no time to tell me what he's thinking.

"Then what?" I shrug. Curious where *we* go from here.

"You ask a lot of a fucking questions." He raises a brow, his tone un-amused.

"Is that a problem? To ask questions?" I tilt my head to the side. He rubs at his chin, his long caramel colored hair falling into his face.

"It is when I don't have the answers, especially the ones you're looking for, Dirty Bird," he replies honestly, and that slice in my side begins to burn.

"Has Raven come to see me?" I ask, trying to sit up. Felix shakes his head and I can't help the look of confusion that crosses my face. Why wouldn't she come see me?

Noticing my confusion, Felix stiffens. "What aren't you telling me?"

Taking a long breath, I rub at my forehead nervously. "She checked that room and said it was clear—"

"Yeah, you told me when you were half drugged up yesterday," he informs.

"So, is she just a shitty cop, or did she set me up?" I ask myself rather than state to Felix.

Felix's shoulders rise as if he's about to explode with rage, his thick brows slicing inward.

"Let's get you out of here, and I'll look into it," he mutters with so much force I can tell he's ready to draw blood. Something warm surfaces knowing he'd go to lengths for me, but then again I don't want to be the reason for another blood bath. Besides, I can handle my own shit.

"Felix," I shake my head with hesitation. "Don't. I'm just paranoid. Obviously I've been hanging around you too much, scared everyone is out to get me." I roll my eyes for effect.

Felix stands, looking down at me with heated eyes. They pin me where I lay, making my body come back alive in a heartbeat.

"That's because I've learned from personal experience to trust very few people in my life. You get to throwing your loyalty around too easily and that is when you get stabbed in the back."

My eyes snap to his, his words making so much sense. Especially since I was just literally stabbed.

Holding the crook of my arm, he pulls the IV out and presses his finger down where a trickle of blood tries to escape. A slight sting races up my arm from the IV being torn out.

"What are you doing?" I ask with alarm.

"Getting you out of here," Felix informs as if it's obvious.

He throws the blanket off of me and I notice I'm wearing a hospital gown and it covers very little. My thighs are showing, and it dips down low to my breast. I try to pull on it, but it does no good.

"Shouldn't a nurse check me out, or I need to sign some papers?" I squirm.

Felix flinches with my suggestion. Like I'm being ridiculous.

"Fuck that. I'm taking you back to my club, to my bed, and nobody is stopping me from that," he retorts.

He slides his arms under my body and lifts me from the bed. I wrap an arm around his neck and pull him in close out of instinct. The feel of his warm, hard body against mine is all I need to know that I'm safe. His strong scent of leather and spice bringing me home.

Felix steps outside my room, and I notice Machete and Gatz standing guard.

"Get the truck, we're leaving," Felix orders, his voice rumbling through my body.

"Um, sir." A concerned nurse rounds the nurse's station. Her hair a frizzy mess, and her Looney Tunes scrubs wrinkled. "You can't just take her without a doctor's consent!"

Felix's grip tightens around my body as he holds me close. He lowers his head, his eyes hooded and daring. Little hairs on the back of my neck stand seeing a darkness cross him. His body stiffens beneath me, and his heartbeat throbs in his temples.

"You going to stop me?" Felix growls, challenging her. The nurse stops, her hands fumbling with the bottom hem of her top as she looks the other way. "I didn't think so," Felix clips.

He stomps toward the entrance, and I can't help but nuzzle the crook of his neck.

There is nowhere else I would rather be.

It both disturbs me and excites me.

FELIX

When Machete parks the SUV, I scoop Alessandra up and slide out of the back seat. We don't even make it to the front door before Jillian rushes out in complete panic.

"Oh my God, Alessandra, I was so worried. Me and your mother wanted to come, but they wouldn't let us…" I step passed her into the club, and she continues to follow us blubbering in tears. Her mother is trying to dance with Mac, who is standing on the couch with a broom to keep her back. I can't help but smirk at the scene, until my eyes fall on Zeek standing by the bar with his arms crossed, eyeing me. That look of hardness, judging me as I hold onto Alessandra. I return the 'fuck you' stare, and make my way down the hall where I run into Machete.

"Get the doctor to come check her out, make sure to get whatever fucking meds we need and shit," I tell him.

"On it," he gives a curt nod.

"Are you okay?" Jillian asks, stepping up behind us.

"I'm fine, Jillian. I promise," Alessandra tries to soothe Jillian over my shoulder, as I ain't fucking stopping. Making it to my door, I kick it open and shut it. Locking it.

"You couldn't even stop and let me talk to her?" Alessandra snaps hatefully. I glare at her tone.

"Nope." Stopping means questioning. Questions from my

boys wanting to know why I'm stuck to Alessandra like a lovestruck boyfriend, and I ain't ready to find the answer to that.

Slowly I lay her on the bed and pull out of my cut and jeans. Grabbing my shirt, I tug it over my head and slide in beside her, tearing the cheap hospital gown off of her. Her cheeks turn a shade of red, but I don't give a fuck about her humility. It took everything I had not to slide into that shitty hospital bed and feel her skin against mine. To feel her heartbeat and know she was going to be okay.

Hovering over her, my hands slide along her bare arms, my lips and nose brushing against her silky skin. The smell of honey and coconut taking me to a paradise that is in the sun and not cold darkness that has become my life.

Sliding my hands along her side, I stop at her wound and slowly lower my head. Gently kissing around it as if the remedy to her pain is held in my lips. Her fingers tangle into my hair in a caring matter as I continue to kiss her body.

"Felix," she whispers.

"Yeah?" I glance up at her.

"Us, this? What does it mean?" I'm so sick of that question, as I don't fucking know and don't want to think about it. It scares me because my biggest fear is I don't deserve this, and it will be taken away from me.

"That's what I plan to figure out, and we ain't leaving this bed until we do," I tell her, sliding up beside her I pull her into me. Her ass fits into my body's curve perfectly like she was made for me.

Who knew someone so wrong for me, so opposite would break everything I ever knew. Demolish the code of Outlaw and rebrand the criminal that I am.

Two days later

Music from the bar is loud and thumping "Wrong Side of Heaven" by Five Finger Death Punch. It makes me wonder how Jillian gets those kids to sleep with all of the noise. But that isn't what wakes me up. Alessandra crying does.

"No, I don't want to!" she wails, and I take a hand right to the mouth.

"What the fuck?" I sit up and find her face clenched tight with fear, and she's covered in sweat.

"Black Bird," I whisper loudly, trying to shake her awake. She begins to slap at me, screaming no, and I become frustrated.

I take a fist to the jaw, a knee to the chest, and slap to the face in the process of trying to wake her from her nightmare.

I grasp her by the throat to pin her down from hitting me and it's as if I just injected her with a sedative, she relaxes instantly in my hold. My brows furrow in confusion as I stare at her. Her eyes now open and looking up at me. It seems every time I grab her here it's as if she gives me complete control of herself. It has to be related to her past.

Shifting next to her, my hand still on her throat I rest my head back on my pillow.

These feelings I have for her are strong. I don't know if it's love because I've never felt it before. I don't want to be in love. Nobody will look at me with fear, but as a man who is pussy whipped.

I am not that, nor will I ever be. I am in control, strong, and the fucking vice president of the Sin City Outlaws.

"I don't love you," I whisper into the back of her head, making sure she knows I'm not the prince to save her from her fucked up world. I'm the villain in her world, and that needs to be very clear.

"I don't love you back," she mutters.

NINE
ALESSANDRA

Waking up a hand is tight around my collarbone and I feel on cloud nine. Safe, and like I'm home. Felix stirs next to me and removes his hand from my throat and it's as if I was suddenly dumped into an ice bath with the void that is left behind.

Why I feel like that is scary, I shouldn't like to be held around the throat like that. I can't help it though, when he does it, I just feel instantly safe. I don't have to pretend to be in control because I'm giving it to him. I trust him.

Using both hands he runs them down his face and rolls onto his side. His sleepy eyes finding mine.

"Do you remember the nightmare you had last night?" he asks softly. I furrow my brows not remembering waking up at all.

"No."

"Really?" He tilts his head to the side with disbelief.

I shake my head. "No, I don't remember anything. Why what happened?" God, I hope I didn't say anything embarrassing.

"You just started hitting me and yelling. I felt like I was in the ring with WWE or something," he chuckles, and I can't help but giggle.

"I get nightmares a lot, they're always the same," I mutter, tracing a tattoo of a skull on his arm.

"What are they about?"

I shrug. "A little girl. She's covered in blood, and scared, pushed to kill. Sometimes the little girl is jumping off a cliff," I explain. They seem so real and familiar that I'm usually sick the next day after an episode. Felix's face hardens, and he looks straight up at the ceiling.

"You okay?" I ask. His head snaps to mine, a look of confliction clouding his eyes.

"Yeah," he mumbles, his tone of voice thick with emotion.

Rubbing his scruffy chin, I can't help but want to know more about this man.

"Why do they call you Felix?" I ask with a smile, and he turns his head my way.

"Why do you want to know?" he replies with a husky tone that has my nipples budding with longing.

I shrug, as I casually circle that tattoo of a praying lady on his bicep.

"My mother was a club hang around, a slut if I'm being honest. She had a Felix The Cat tattoo on her lower back my dad said. When she had me she left me at the hospital with not so much as a name. She wrote my dad's name and number on the birth certificate though, and he came and got me; called me Felix," he tells the story that has my brows furrowing with anger and sympathy. There is no emotion in his tone, as if he's detached from the most important thing that makes him... him.

"My dad said I look like my mother in the face," he whispers, and I take notice he doesn't have the Italian look that Zeek does. His brows and long hair are thick, but his skin is of a lighter color.

"So it's true, you were raised by the club," I state rather than ask. They said one of them was raised by the club and has no respect for the law or the well-being of others more so than any of the other men.

"Is that something you learned in the academy?" he smarts with a huff.

I silently laugh. "Actually yeah. It's kind of crazy they make us learn about you guys before we can pass, but actually seeing you guys up close, I can say they are wrong about you guys," I mutter softly.

"No, they're not. It's just very few get to see a side nobody else does," he exhales, before running his hands down his face as if he didn't mean to say that out loud. I can tell by the way he's tensing he's done talking about him.

"How is your side?" He pulls the sheets down and inspects my wound. My stomach knots when I notice I'm still naked. I forgot he tore the hospital gown from my body yesterday and pulled me into him like he'd been dying to have me by his side for days.

"It itches, and is a little sensitive," I inform, watching the beady strings snake in and out of my side.

Felix slides out of bed, and his hard clenched butt cheeks come into full view. Anything painful that might have been on my mind disappears as a blush of desire heats my skin. Rubbing my thighs together I bite my bottom lip and think of anything else but sex.

"I have to go to the station today, make my statement about what happened," I tell him.

"I'll take you," he tells me rather than asks. I can't help but roll my eyes at his controlling attitude. Same ol' Felix.

He bends over, messing with the radio and Seether "Broken" thumps through the speakers. I haven't heard this song in forever. Felix disappears into the bathroom and comes out with a tube of Vaseline.

Kneeling on the floor, he leans over the mattress and dabs some goo on the tip of his finger and slowly, and very carefully applies it to my side. His eyes focused and strong as is hands make me feel more than better.

Suddenly the door is opened and both Felix and I jerk our attention to the door.

Gia stands there in a black Harley shirt and frayed shorts. Her eyes wide and angry as she stares at us. I grab the sheet to cover myself, but Felix just turns his attention back to my wound.

"Get out," he states with force.

"Why?" she asks. "Why her?" Gia's voice clogs with emotion.

Felix sighs and stands. Grabbing his junk he pins her with a deathly stare.

"I said get out," he warns.

"Look at this. Look at you!" she cries, pointing at me.

"What? What is it you think you see?" Felix barks, making me jump where I sit.

"You care for her. I've never seen you look or touch someone like you do her." Tears slip down her face and I almost feel sorry for her.

"You need to go," Felix repeats, grabbing the door. Gia puts her foot in the door. "Do you love her?" Felix kicks her foot out of the way and slams the door.

I swallow the lump in my throat and avert my eyes back to the bed.

He struts back to the bed, and kneels down.

His eyes pull to mine, and a knowing look crosses his face.

His hands slide down to my thighs, and he jerks me to the edge of the bed. I laugh, wrapping my arms around his neck.

Pressing his lips to mine, I kiss him back, lost in the smell of him, his hard touch, and the good music.

This feels too right who cares if anyone outside this room thinks it's wrong.

He swings us and lays my back onto the floor, my legs straddling around his hard waist. The tip of his throbbing cock brushes against my clit and I suck in a tight breath. A thunderstorm developing between my legs from the anticipation.

Running my nails down his hard chest, I lean forward and grab his sexy nipple between my teeth. His lips against my neck he hisses from the pressure I apply on the delicate skin.

Pulling his lips to my mouth his mouth fits mine perfectly. The warmth of his body throwing my heartbeat into orbit. He slips his hard cock inside of me slowly, and attentively. Dark eyes never leaving mine as he goes as deep as he can inside. His hips slowly make love to me as his tongue mimics his thrusting torso. He stretches me, fills me, and takes me away from my pain. When Felix and I are together like this, it's as if we aren't even on the same planet as everyone else. It's just him and me in our own world. No one matters, and everything blurs. He's an outlaw in public and a master in the bedroom.

The sound of his heartbeat grounds me, the brush of his lips across my skin comforts me, the feel of his rough hands along my body claiming me as his.

It's an emotion all on its own. One I've grown addicted to and will be broken and misplaced without.

His long hair falls from his face and tickles my collarbone. Taking my attention from his chest to his head I fist his silky hair as I ride his large cock. The floor bites into my back, the dirt rubbing into my skin as I'm shuffled back and forth. The heat of his body on mine, and the feel of bliss between my legs a piece of heaven I never want to end. If I die, this is how I want to go out. Just like this.

He places a hand by my head on the floor, his arms flexing as he holds himself up. He's so strong and sexy I want him all to myself, I want to be his. Wrapping my hands around his back I dig my nails in, pulling him closer to me as tingles begin to ignite in my core. My breathing picks up, and pressure builds to heights of pleasure I can't explain. His brows furrow, his rhythm picking up as he's about to come with me.

My mouth opens into a shape of an 'O', and he gently places his hand on my collarbone and

I free fall into ecstasy, giving every ounce that I am to Felix.

A knock on the door has us snap out of our world, and the door is jerked open. Again.

"GODDAMN IT!" Felix roars, trying to cover my naked body with his own.

"Church, brother," Machete informs.

Felix snatches the sheet off the bed and throws it over me in a matter of seconds.

"GET THE FUCK OUT!" Felix points at him with a sharp finger. His tone conveying he's not to be argued with.

Machete chuckles, not taking the tone of Felix seriously as his eyes linger on me a second longer than necessary before closing the door.

"I'll be back," he whispers against my lips.

"Okay," I smile, and he gently pulls out of me.

As I watch him get dressed I wonder when the hell we became this, what I allowed myself to fall into. As I am falling for Felix, and I didn't want to. I never wanted to fall for any man.

I'm scared of being hurt, scarred, and broken hearted. One-night stands don't come with shattered hearts, or feelings.

But this, whatever it is. It's real and happening whether I want it to or not.

It's out of my control, and that is a first for me.

Felix is showing me how to live, and I'm going to show him how to love. Even if it kills us.

FELIX

Sitting at the table I can smell her on my skin, still feel her legs wrapped around me and it's taking everything I have not to stand up from this table and go back to her. I can still feel her pussy squeezing around my cock, and her nails digging into my back.

I've tasted Alessandra, and I can't forget her flavor no matter how hard I try.

"Did you hear me, Felix?" Zeek asks, and I snap to.

"What?"

"Salvatore at the casino wants to see us again. I need my VP with me," he tells me.

"What about Alessandra, she has to go to the station today and make a statement?" I ask, trying not to come off like a little bitch, but it's failing.

"Gatz will go with her and will bring her back as soon as she is done. I need you with me, end of!" Zeek sneers. Rolling my fingers into my palm I clench my fists tight, wanting so badly to punch Zeek in his arrogant mouth. I think he forgets the shit this club went through for Jillian.

"Fine," I mutter, pushing away from the table. I swear to God if Gatz fucks this up I'll find that purple dildo and shove it up his ass.

Mac steps in front of me and hands me a phone.

"What's this?"

"Give it to Alessandra. It's got a tracker on it, and nobody but I can trace it," he explains. "Just a precaution," he continues with a proud smile.

Alessandra wasn't given a phone with her belongings, so that means someone at the department has it. Probably that Raven bitch, which I don't trust. It's her fault Alessandra was nearly killed. Even Alessandra is questioning where Raven's loyalty lies.

"Hey, can you run Alessandra's partner Raven in your computer shit?"

He folds his arms and looks at me offended. "Of course, why what is up?"

"I don't trust that bitch, I want everything you can find on her," I tell him. "Everything!" I reiterate.

"Yeah, I'll see what I can dig up." He shrugs.

"Thanks, man."

Stepping back into the room Alessandra is dressed and putting her dark hair into a messy ponytail. My chest squeezes wanting to pull her to me and rip her clothes off, something so beautiful should never be covered and I would come through on that deed if duty didn't call.

"I can't go with you to the station. Zeek needs me, so Gatz is going to take you," I tell her before taking a seat on the bed.

She giggles, and pulls my hands from my knees, sitting on my lap.

"You say it like you're jealous," she says with a smile. She's right, I am, and I don't like it. Not at all. I want to lock her away so nobody can see her but me. Nobody can smell how sweet she is, but me. Nobody can have her, but me.

Sliding my hand up her back I fist her hair hard.

"I'm not a jealous man, but I find myself claiming you." The words take me by surprise, but they're true. She is mine, and I won't take it back. Her eyes flash longingly and she cups my cheek softly. "Do you have a problem with that?" I question.

Her eyes flick between mine before a smirk crosses her gorgeous face.

"I don't think I have much say in the matter," she laughs. Leaning forward I rest my lips against her, that unfamiliar feeling in my chest making me feel a million things at once again.

"That's because you don't. Neither of us does," I mutter against her plush lips. My eyes on hers, and the softness she conveys making me feel vulnerable. "I don't love you," I tell her, needing to hear myself say it.

Pulling back, she raises a brow. "I don't love you back."

I smirk, not fully believing her. The way her hand swayed toward mine in her darkest hour I'd say she cares for me, she just doesn't want to admit it. She's a strong creature, like me. Falling in love feels like a weakness as we can't control it and we control everything.

She slides off my lap, her fine ass swaying back and forth and I can't help but give it a squeeze. Loving the way it feels in my hands. It's soft but toned. My dick jumps wanting to stick it in her ass, see her body arch as I fill her.

"I gotta go." She looks over her shoulder, batting her eyes and my gaze jumps from her ass to her eyes.

"Take this." I hand her the phone.

She frowns holding it. "I have a phone."

"Raven has your phone, and I don't trust her. Take this one, Mac has it souped-up and shit," I insist. She shrugs and tucks it in her back pocket.

"Fine, only because you're annoying me," she replies seriously, before stepping out of the room. That defying mouth, the smell of her lingering in the room. What the fuck is happening to me.

"I don't love her. I don't love her. I don't love her," I whisper to myself, thudding my fist against the closed door. I can't love her. I don't deserve her. I've done nothing but been selfish and greedy my whole life, and finding her hasn't changed me, it made those attributes worse.

I'm a fucking convict and will escort anyone within distance to hell with me… and I'm willing to take Alessandra first fucking class.

ALESSANDRA

Stepping out of the room I find my mother whistling happily and sweeping the floor. She's wearing jeans and a Sin City Outlaws shirt. Her hair in a black bandana. She looks good, and happy.

"Hey Mom!" I say cheerfully, not sure if she's in a moment of clarity or not. She looks over her shoulder and lights up.

"Hey! I was going to come see you but with that big ol biker in there I didn't know what I'd walk in on," she winks before laughing. My cheeks turn red, and I rub my neck anxiously. "How are you?" she asks, touching my shoulder tenderly.

"Better, but my stitches feel tight." I twist my torso with a frown on my body.

"Yeah, your daddy never did like those much either," she informs, and the smile crossing my face is bittersweet. I'm still torn thinking of him not being my father.

Mac walks out of a room in nothing but a low-rise pair of

jeans. He looks at us before doing a double take, his eyes wide as he walks as fast as he can into the bathroom across the hall.

Mom fans herself with her hand not holding the broom.

"That man reminds me so much of your father," she exhales, and I can't help but laugh.

"I better go freshen up." She winks at me before disappearing into another room. I don't even know what to say to that.

Walking down the hall Gia starts down the hallway. She's wearing short shorts and a ripped AC/DC shirt. She'd be pretty if she wasn't after Felix. My shoulders tense, and my resting bitch face immediately falls into place.

She stops in front of me, her hand on her hip.

"You're still here?" she sneers. "You don't belong here, and you know it."

My brows narrow in on her, taking a step toward her. I'm done with the games, and if it means I have to tear her hair extensions out to make my claim on Felix, then I will.

"Felix is mine, and if he hasn't made that clear, let me. If you so much as flip your hair in his direction I will make your face looks like your botched tit job." My eyes fall to her unleveled breasts before meeting her gaze. Her mouth drops, a gasp escaping.

"You're a cop. No matter what you think you have you'll never be apart of this—"

"I will kill you and I promise you, nobody will find your body," I threaten, my words not only catching me by surprise but Gia's jaw falls open with disbelief.

"Get the fuck out of here Gia!" Mac barks from behind her, making her jump where she stands.

Her eyes begin to fill with tears as she looks at Mac with pleading eyes.

"You heard me, go before Felix finds out you're fucking

harassing his bitch." Mac rubs at his chin, eyeing her up and down. "Now if you need someone's dick to keep you company, I'd be more than happy to oblige you," he winks, and Gia lights up like a fucking Christmas tree.

"Wow, you really are a ho," I mutter, but she either doesn't hear me or doesn't care because she slips into the next room with a smile on her face. It makes me wonder if the men share medicine with their crabs, seeing how they share their women.

I give Mac a tight-lipped smile and exhale the hostility brewing inside of me. "I could have handled her, but thank you."

He scoffs. "I saw how you handled Dolly, I can't have you beating up all our ass around here," he chuckles, and I laugh.

He steps past me, the smell of cologne strong, the tattoos all over his arms catching.

"Oh and I just want to say, I've met some scary motherfuckers in my life, but your mother takes the goddamn cake, Alessandra," he says seriously.

I shrug and continue down the hallway.

"Be scared if she busts out the pepper spray," I tip him.

"She has pepper spray?" he says with dread.

Turning to walk backward so I can see him, I nod. "Oh yeah, we don't go anywhere without it," I reply as casually as I can, and the look on his face has me nearly bursting at the seams with laughter.

Getting into the SUV with Gatz I notice the kid from the other day, Bishop, hauling boxes in the back door of the club. He looks clean, and on a mission. He looks up, his eyes catching me staring and he stops in his tracks and give a lift of the chin. I wink at him, a smile spreading across my face seeing him here.

"You sent him didn't you?" I turn where I stand finding

Jillian smiling at me with Sam on her hip.

"He needs a home, a brotherhood that will protect him," I explain to her.

She sighs, leaning against the car.

"I get it, you always did go about things different than the book," she chuckles. I look down, not sure how much she knows about me going off the rulebook of the department. In fact, I don't know how much more of the rulebook I can follow or want to follow. Being here the short time I have I've started to question what I really want in life. Did I just join the force because of my father and I didn't know where to go in life? Because it's starting to feel that way.

"How are you doing?" She eyes my side, and I shrug, drawing circles into the dust of the SUV.

The metal of the car warm beneath the pad of my finger.

"I'll live," I smile. She leans in and hugs me, surprising me.

"I know it's a part of the job, but goddamn you scared me," she whispers in my ear. Baby Sam starts to cry being smooshed in-between us and she pulls back. My eyes prick with tears and I have to look away or I might cry at how much she cares for me.

"Stop it hooker, you're going to make me cry," I swat at her. Suddenly Mac comes running out of the clubhouse, a look of fear on his face as he looks over his shoulder. Probably running from my mother.

"I see Mom is enjoying it here." I smile, wiping a tear that escaped. Jillian shrugs.

"She has it bad for Mac that's for sure," Jillian laughs, "But, she really seems to enjoy herself here."

"My mom happy, I don't think I've seen that in a long time," I answer solemnly. Done with heart to heart I open the passenger door.

"I'll be back, and we should catch up," I offer.

"Deal, now hurry back!" she hollers, bouncing Sam on her hip.

Sitting next to Gatz in the SUV I notice he doesn't smell like the rest of the men around the club. He is... clean. His clothes are spotless, and not a wrinkle in sight. He's definitely different.

"Why are you looking at me like that?" he asks, keeping his eye on the road.

"It's just, you're different than the rest of the Outlaws is all." I shrug, my cheeks turning red from being caught staring.

"I *am* different," he replies, glancing at me before returning his stare back to the road.

"Why?" I ask curiously.

"Some say I'm gay," he shrugs.

I raise a brow. "Are you?"

He doesn't reply, as he just keeps his eyes on the road. He's so clean and sexy. I bet he's gay.

"You can't tell me can you, because it's against code?" I ask, but he doesn't answer. His Adam's apple bobs, as his grip tightens on the steering wheel and I know I hit home.

"I won't tell anyone, but if they really are your brothers... they'll understand," I advise. That's not always true though. I've heard of gangs cutting members dicks off, and banning them from their gang for being gay, or a certain religion.

He scoffs, rubbing his chin with his thumb as he continues to drive. Not giving away anything.

Arriving to the station I give a tight-lipped smile as I climb out of the car.

"Hopefully this won't take long," I say on an exhale.

He shrugs as if he's indifferent and pulls out his phone. Relaxing back into the seat.

I shake my head. Men, whether they're gay or not, they cannot grasp communication, I swear.

Entering the station it smells of coffee and is busy as usual. I give a nod to a couple of the regulars and head to the dressing room. I need to change into my uniform. I feel naked being here without wearing it.

Pulling my hair out of the back of my uniform shirt, I glance in the mirror and find Raven leaning up against the brick that makes up the shower stall.

"Oh, hey," I smile. She's not in uniform, which I find weird. I've never seen her not in uniform before, so it takes me aback. Her hair is down, and she's wearing a black shirt and jeans.

"Hey," she says with no humor. "You look like you survived," she says bitterly. I raise a brow at her tone. A little hurt she didn't come see me in the hospital. Not that it's required of her, I just thought being her partner she would be concerned.

"Did someone shit in your cereal?" I sneer in return.

She scoffs at my statement. "I have your phone. Do you want it?" she changes the subject.

"Yeah, I have a lot of pictures and stuff on there." She turns without saying a word, and I follow her out to the back lot where the cruisers are kept. I wonder if I said something to upset her. She opens the passenger door and gestures her hand to the console.

"Thanks for keeping it for me, if it was put into evidence it would probably be cracked or—"

Before I can finish my statement a blinding white light slams into my head knocking me into the car face first. Losing consciousness everything turns black, and I instantly wonder what the fuck I got myself into.

FELIX

Sitting at the desk, Salvatore continues to puff on his cigar, eyeing Zeek and I over the smoke dancing between us. I can't pinpoint the type of cigar but it's strong and more than likely expensive. The desk shines as if it has been recently shined, and the windows are so clean I can see my reflection from here. He's made himself comfortable here, and I find it unsettling. I find everything about this fucker off, and I'm done playing puppet. Blood will be shed, and the vengeance of an untold war will start before I leave this room tonight.

"Seems your club has survived the target that was placed on your back," he replies smugly.

"Didn't notice there was one," I reply arrogantly.

He chuckles. "I'm sure you didn't. I've called you guys here today to settle a score. You don't want to be our muscle, that's your loss. However, what about doing business?" he offers.

"Depends what it is," Zeek crosses his arms.

"We will call off the heat if you agree to ten percent."

"Of what?" I ask, getting tired of his vagueness.

"Us letting you stay on the strip of course." He laughs maniacally.

"You're trying to shake us down?" I raise a brow, standing. I've had enough of this shit.

"You need our protection boys, it's clear to see." He holds his hands out, his voice serious. "The Bosses aren't happy with you guys if you remember?"

Quickly I pull my gun from my waistband and aim it at his head. Two of his men instantly pull their guns in my directions. Zeek remains sitting, calm.

"I have a message for your boss," I tell him, and his eyes widen. "No deal." I change the aim of my gun and pull the trigger. A bullet slamming into one of his guard's heads, just as Zeek puts a bullet in the other's head. They both fall to the ground, their blood staining the floor.

Salvatore stands, his face red and flustered. He's scared shitless that we were so bold to have killed two of the mafia's guards, but maybe now he will get the fucking hint of who he is fucking with.

Salvatore sits back in his seat and takes a drag of his cigar.

"I'll deliver your message," he replies eerily calm.

"Good," I quip.

ALESSANDRA

Waking up my mouth is dry, my head hurts, and my face feels wet. The smell of damp dirt and the familiar smell of old blood lingers around me.

Reaching out to touch my sore head my hand hits something hard. Looking up, I notice I'm in a cage of some sort.

"Hello?" I scream, shaking the cage, but nobody answers. My head rings, and the dry blood mats my hair. Fear begins to sink its teeth into my chest and I start to hyperventilate.

This cage, this place, it's familiar. But how?

"Brown 5, you are not a little girl, and you are not a human. You are a weapon, do you understand?"

Pulling my knees into myself my hair shielded my face from the man pacing in front of my cage. His black hat was pulled down so far I couldn't even see his eyes. Just a broad nose, and thick lips.

"Yes sir," I responded meekly. Not sure the difference between a little girl and what I am anyway.

I shake my head of the image and gasp for air as if I was just shoved underwater and couldn't breathe. I grab at the bars in front of me, my knuckles white from the grip.

This is all too familiar, little pieces of the nightmares over the years of my life suddenly becoming my reality.

"Starting to piece it together?" The familiar voice of Raven echoes through the dark area before she finally steps into view. A small light bulb swings just above her casting an eerie glow down amongst her.

"I... I can't remember." I blink rapidly, the answer to everything on the tip of my tongue. It's all so familiar, yet strange.

The sound of kids screaming in the cages next to me. Bruises and fights reeling through my head like a bad movie. Swallowing hard I try to resist the thoughts coming through my memory, needing out of this cage, this place.

Wait, I have the phone Felix gave me. Instantly I shove my hand down my back pocket and Raven laughs.

"Yeah, we took that. How dumb do you think we are?" Raven laughs, and my hooded eyes draw to hers.

"You're a fucking traitor," I grit, and she scoffs.

"Speak for yourself, Brown 5." Her calling me Brown 5, hits me like a beaming black light sent from hell.

I used to live here. Fight here. Not live, but survive. Not just me, but lots of kids.

"This is crazy. This isn't real," I mutter, trying to pull it all together. This is just a nightmare, this isn't real.

"It's very real. Iraq, Pakistan, lots of places do what happened here. Taking children from happy homes, ripping them of their memories and personalities, and making them into human weapons," a male voice adds. My head snaps to the right, watching a dark shadow enter into the meek lighting. He's wearing a hat lowered on his head, a dark shirt that is ripped showing hard abs, and black jeans.

A tall man with a black hat hovering over me filters into my memory, and I begin to shake where I sit. He hurt me, starved me, and then cared for me. I don't remember him fully, but the terror wracking through my body tells me I hated him. He's older now, his face wrinkled, and hair grayed. He looks more terrifying now than he does in my nightmares.

"Wh-what is this?" I stutter, looking at Raven through thick steel bars.

"Let me remind you. I'm Black A," she seethes.

Dark memories swirl in my head, flashing behind my eyes. Clutching my head, I lower it trying to slow all the images stringing together behind my eyes. The voices and sounds that weren't there coming forth now.

"You will defeat Black A, or you won't eat dinner. You've defeated her three times, but if you beat her five times in a row the master will put her to rest and you will be the best!" Black Hat explained, a tear slid from the corner of my eyes. I didn't want to hurt her, I didn't want to hurt anyone.

"Enough of that. People cry, weak people cry. You are not people, you are a machine!" he hollers in my face, locking me into my cage, my home.

"Black A," I whisper, everything about her returning. I eye her, my opponent that I was conditioned to forget. My dad - I cringe at the term. I remember him finding me, and the therapy treatments to forget my past, but everything else is a blur. How he became my father, how my life became normal I don't know.

"But you're my partner?" I ask confused.

"I was pushed into being a cop to get close to you, dumbass!" she snaps. Raven, Cross, and Black Hat. All of this was a set-up.

Black Hat hunches down in front of my cage, flicking the lock with his finger effortlessly. Showing me I am his prisoner, that I'm not free.

"What are you going to do now that your man isn't here to protect you?" he sneers, talking about Felix.

"I don't need a man to handle my shit," I mutter, my head lowered, eyes hooded. If I'm released from this cage, I might kill this man. The urge running through my veins is toxic and unpredictable. I can't control the darkness lurking through me when I look at him.

"I broke you once, I can do it again," he threatens. I'm scared, nearly ready to piss myself, but I won't let him know that.

"Fuck you!" I growl. He tilts his head to the side with a look of desire. "You were a child back then, now that you're a woman, that can be arranged in your training, Brown 5," he's smug, and something dark rears its head as I lash out trying to grab him through the bars.

"I'll kill you!" I roar, not sure where the words or anger are coming from.

"You're going to have your work cut out for you." Raven eyes me like a wild animal. It's accurate, I feel like one.

"Yeah, but when she breaks, she will be the one to bring The Sin City Outlaws to their knees. Starting by hitting Zeek right where it hurts, by taking his children," Black Hat informs. "Cross will take over and everything will be back to the way it was."

My head snaps up with his news. "What did you say?"

Hunching over I throw up, my uniform pants painted with warm chunks from the donut I swiped on my way to the locker room. Black Hat laughs deeply, pleased with the terror etching itself into my memory one image at a time.

Cross worked for Frank who used to control the Sin City Outlaws, but I never knew how fucked up the man really was. He is going to take Jillian's kids and do to them exactly what he did to me and Raven.

"I'm going to let Cross know we have her and grab that box of shit you brought to get this started. Watch her closely," Black Hat points at me, and I flip him off in return.

"Don't forget my wine!" Raven hollers after him.

She stands just underneath the light, her arms crossed as she looks at me curiously, angrily. The rookie I thought I knew long gone, and placed with a mysterious dark creature.

"Why are you doing this?" I ask, pushing my emotions to the back of my throat. Raven is free, I am free. Why wouldn't she tell me all of this when she met me and we could work together in finding Cross and these human trafficking rings?

"Because, you were saved and I wasn't!" she screams so loud my ears ring, all of her pent up emotion spilling at once. "You were privileged enough to forget about what happened here, but I wasn't! I will never forget, Brown 5!" she screams, kicking the cage I'm contained in. The rage in her voice, the resentment in her tone, I know she more than hates me.

"You tried to have me killed didn't you?" I eye her, the stitches in my side itching and burning. They are probably pulled apart.

She laughs mockingly. "If I wanted you dead, you would be. That day we were going to take you if fucking dispatch didn't call it in," she informs, and I clamp my eyes shut. I should have listened to my gut, I shouldn't have trusted Raven. Suddenly Raven turns, lifting her shirt revealing a scar in the shape of an X.

"I am Black A, and nothing will change that. Just as you are Brown 5, and always will be. You will remember everything, and hurt just like me, " she informs gravely, my life as I know it vanishing as I know it and replacing with something much darker.

I slide my hand up the back of my shirt, the pad of my finger sliding over the scar on my lower back that is identical to hers.

"This X will remind you that you are branded, that you are stock and replaceable. You are owned, Brown 5. Your parents are no longer, I am your parent your teacher." Clenched eyes I wail as searing hot metal burns into my lower back.

I shake my head of the flashback, willing them to stay forgotten. The darkness creeping through my veins at these memories making me feel cold and bitter.

"This is what we are bred to do, made to do. We were handpicked to be the best criminals in the world. Trained to be lethal, and killed if you're lesser than that." She points at me. "You are my lesser, tainted and weak and I will prove that!" She kicks my cage, and I flinch.

"It's an act of terrorism, Raven, not strength," I explain, trying to dig the world of law enforcement up through all of the broken memories trying to take over.

"Every day I went without food because of you. No shower, or blanket because of you. *You* haunted my dreams and made my nightmares. *You* are the monster that lurks behind a badge without a clue of what you've done and it's not fair!" Her face is red, sweaty, and she is irrational as she releases her pent up aggression.

Black Hat struts back into the room with a box, sliding it onto the table behind Raven.

"Everything okay?" he questions her, and she takes a deep breath.

"Of course, I can handle it," she replies calmly, as if she

didn't just go crazy bitch on me.

"I brought that cheap ass wine you like, thought we could celebrate catching her," Black Hat chuckles.

I rattle the bars, needing out. Feeling suffocated, and hopeless. I can't just sit here and let all of this happen again.

"SOMEONE HELP ME!" I scream so loud my throat bleeds. I know nobody can hear me, but I have to fight back.

"Shut up!" Black Hat throws an empty beer can at me.

"Let me out of here now!" I kick the cage back, not caring of the repercussions.

"That's it," he seethes, turning behind him he grabs something off the table. Being down on the ground I can't see what is on it. Hunching down, he unlocks the cage, and I begin to kick and scratch. Bite and scream. Anything to gain some control and escape. He sits on top of me, the cage so small I'm pinned to the cold ground. Fisting my chin harshly, he dabs something on my lips, and I whimper as a thick warmth coats them. Using both hands, he pinches my lips together, before blowing on them. His dark eyes bringing so many memories to the surface. I close my eyes, not wanting to remember the terror this man brought to my life but it's no use. They fly into place and I feel more like myself than I ever have. It's scary. I feel dangerous, alive, and ruthless.

I was Brown 5, taken from my family to train to be the best killer. I have no life, this was life.

He pushes me back into the cage and slams the door shut, locking it.

Opening my mouth to scream at him I can't. My lips are sealed shut and when I try to pull them apart it tears at the skin brutally.

My wide eyes cut to his and he holds a small tube in between his thumb and forefinger. Super Glue. He fucking glued my lips shut.

"Watch her, I'm going to go take a piss," he orders Raven. When he leaves the room, I pry at my lips, clenching my eyes shut as I peel them apart like layers of an onion. It stings, burns, and I have to stop halfway as tears slip from eyes from the excruciating pain.

"You really are fucking stupid," Raven taunts, watching me tear my lips apart. It's just pain, I can do this.

Taking a deep breath, I bite my cheek and try to pull my inner Brown 5 to the surface. A warrior not scared of pain, but a survivor. Trying again I jerk at my lips and the soft skin of my lips tear and bleed, but finally they part slowly.

Sobbing, I wipe the blood splitting from my bottom lip with the back of my hand.

Raven eyes me like an animal that just did a trick, amazed. She may hate me, but she looks up to me. I can tell.

"I remember most of everything, Raven. I remember how scared I was back then, how hungry I was, I was in that shit with you, and..." My head falls, wishing so hard I could change what happened but I can't. Not wanting to remember the hurt and pain I caused others just like me.

I'm a fucking monster and went around with my head held high knowing I was different but not the depths of it.

Looking up through blurry eyes, lips bleeding, I sigh at a loss for words.

"I am not your enemy, he is," I point where Black Hat went. Her hands drop as she eyes the room Black Hat went in. Her body tensing. "Cross is who took everything from us, and broke us." I tremble with anger, with pain.

"No, you went on living a normal life. Sunday church, a cheesy family. I've been drowning in pain this whole time," she states and a crack of emotion shows. I slipped past her mask of control, and this is my chance to work her. To get out of here.

"I would have taken you with me if I had the choice," sympathy laced in my tone. "I would have taken everyone," I gesture toward the other cages, and her eyes flash with an unknown look.

"It's not too late, you can have normal. Have a family, start over. If I can do it, you can do it." I shrug.

She hunches down, eyeing me with softer eyes. "I still remember my parents, do you?" she asks with glossy eyes. My head falls, and no matter how hard I dig... I don't see them in my heart.

"I don't, but I wish I did," I cry, tears stinging my raw lips.

"It's the only thing I hang onto, my mom and dad. The memories of us before my life was turned into..." she shakes her head. "I'll never escape this hell," she whispers.

"You can escape now, Raven," I coax her, and her head snaps to mine. "You didn't have control last time, you do now," I continue hoping to rub her down.

"I..." she stumbles on her words, her eyes filling with tears. "I've hated you my entire life, and thought about what I would do to you given the chance." She hangs her head, a tear slipping down her cheek. "And now all I want to do is let you go." Her voice thick with emotion. "Why?" she shrugs.

"Do it, let me go, and we can fight this together, Raven." I jump at the bars, reaching through I cup her hand. It's cold and hard, anything you would expect a human to have voided. Her eyes peer up at mine.

"No," she grunts. I blink. No what? No, she won't let me go? Or no we won't fight this?

Standing, she grabs something from the table, and bends back down, unlocking the lock. She looks at me with sad eyes. She's so broken, so hurt and confused she doesn't know what she wants. She just wants to be loved, belong somewhere. I know, because I remember the feeling. If this whole experience brought anything back, it was that cold, searing feeling of not belonging. Dropping the key to the ground, she whimpers before slinking out of the room like a ghost.

Oh my God, I'm free. I'm free. Quickly I unlace the lock holding the door to the cage and push the gate open just as Black Hat walks into the room.

"Where do you think you're going?" He rushes at me and I quickly stand and kick him in the face. His head whips to the side, but it doesn't slow him. He grabs ahold of me and slams my head into the table. A bright light flashes behind my eyes, my head throbbing painfully. I notice a rusty screwdriver lays ahead on the rickety table. I reach for it, but it's just out of reach. *Fuck!* Using my tiptoes I push forward, and my fingers tickle the metal that makes up the straight edge.

The animal in me shakes its cage, roaring to be released at full throttle. I'm not sure what I'm scared of more. Letting the shadows of my past in, or letting my monster out. If I let this darkness seep from the cracks of my soul, there will be no putting it back. I will not be Alessandra, but a mixture of Brown 5 and Alessandra.

Black Hat grips me around the neck, and my body wants to relax into his hold, give him control. He is the reason I act the way I do when Felix touches me there. It was how he controlled me in training. Furrowing my brows, I push past the urge to relent. One man controls me, and that is Felix.

Using all my might I grasp the screwdriver, fisting it, I turn in Black Hat's hold. His grip tightening on my neck to the point I can't breathe. His beady eyes smiling back at me as he squeezes the life out of me.

Taking a deep breath, I let the terror of that little girl

trapped in a cage... out.

Swinging my hand back I slam the straight edge screwdriver into his back until it hits bone. He screams, and backhands me off the table. My face throbs, and pain licks up my temple. Mid fall I grab the box of contents sitting on the table before falling to the ground. A bottle of wine, corkscrew, Taser, leash, and cattle prod falling next to me. He hollers and cries trying to withdraw the tool from his back.

Jerking it free he comes at me with it and I grab the bottle of wine as it's closer and slam it against his head. Knocking him to the ground.

Shifting onto all fours, I climb on top of his back and drive the bottle into his skull one more time. The impact of glass and bone vibrating through my hand just as it breaks in my hold. The smell of strawberries and blood wafting around me. "You corrupted me, and now you're going to die by the hand of the demon you created," I cry with pain not related to my injuries but the hurt that has been buried so long and just now pulling itself from the grave. He reaches for the corkscrew that fell out of the box that's just feet away, and I topple over him to get it first.

Reaching it before him, I place the screw between my fingers and slam it into his neck. It doesn't lodge all the way so I twist it into his skin and blood sprays with every spin of my wrist. He screams, and bucks beneath me as I dig the corkscrew into his main artery. Hooking my legs around him I ride him like a fucking bull, taking his life with a goddamn smile on my face. Accepting my past, my future, the now. I'm killing the nightmare that lingers in every little girl's head, and destroying the master behind the monster that lingers under their bed.

Gritting my teeth, a dark rush envelopes my soul. Nurture

vs nature losing.

Blood sprays over my uniform as I twist the cork all the way in. Crimson painting a canvas of life on my chest. I scream and roar like an animal, tears slipping from my eyes as I take Black Hat's life.

He goes limp falling to the ground, and I release my hold on him. Straddling his back I stand on shaky legs. Blood dripping from my fingertips as I look around the hell that created me. My dad is probably rolling over in his grave right now but it was either I accept who I am, or Cross and them do this to others all over again.

Stepping over the dead body, I decide to go the way Raven went, hoping for an exit.

I should let her escape, but now that the beast is released. The reaper is on a mission, and I'm going to tear her broken soul from her chest. Taking out the trash of Vegas one criminal at a time.

This world has enough heroes. It needs a hybrid. Half hero, half villain.

FELIX

Looking at the clock, I begin to get nervous. Alessandra should be back by now. It's dark, and the station is closed for the most part. I'm going to call Gatz and see what the hold-up is.

A knock at the door takes me from my phone. "Hey man, we got problems," Zeek says solemnly. The hairs on my neck stand on end, and I jump from my chair.

"What?"

Gatz steps into view, his face pale.

"Alessandra went into the station, and never came out," he informs with a shaky voice.

Stomping forward I grab him by the neck and slam him up against the door with more force than I recognize.

"What the fuck do you mean she didn't come out?"

"I went in there hours later and they said she never came in to give her statement," he explains. Zeek grabs at my arm, trying to get me to release Gatz, but the fear in me has me tightening my grip. "You were supposed to protect her!" I yell in his face.

"I know!" he shouts back, regret deep in his voice.

I let him go, my shoulder rising and falling with rage.

Jillian pushes past the boys, her face red. "Where is she?!" She's irate, emotional.

"I don't know!" Gatz replies emotionally. "I'm sorry," he hangs his head, his fingers running through his hair.

"Mac!" Jillian screams, and the babies wake in the back room from the commotion.

"Sup?" Mac asks, chewing on a straw, obviously oblivious to what is going on.

"Alessandra is missing," I feed him in quickly.

"I'll trace the phone!" Mac points at me. Eyeing Zeek, I step past him and follow Mac to his computer. I'm not saying this is Zeek's fault, but I should've taken Alessandra to do her statement. I fucking knew it.

Mac types, clicks, and furrows his brows at a bunch of nonsense popping up on his screen.

"Hurry the fuck up!" I snap. A GPS pops up, and a little pink dot blinks almost out of the city limits. Pushing off the table I head to my room, jerk the closet door open and grab my semi-automatic.

I'm about to rain this city in blood and vengeance. I'm going to retaliate, and reign mayhem.

"Hey man, you gotta chill out bro," Zeek says following behind me. The amount of concern in his voice annoying me. If this was Jillian, he'd already be pulling all of our men and weapons.

"Fuck you," I growl pushing past him. He grabs my arm and pushes me up against the wall and I swing at him, but he ducks.

"If this were Jillian this wouldn't even be up for debate. So why is Alessandra?" I yell in his face.

"It's not, but I don't want to see my best friend, and family killed because he's so fucking distracted!" he screams back.

I take a breath, knowing he's coming from a good place. Scratching my temple with my gun, I eye him.

"I'm not distracted, just the opposite, brother," I tell him firmly.

Stomping through the clubhouse I make my way to my bike, my only mission is saving Black Bird.

"I'm coming with you, brother," Machete says, pulling the chamber back on his gun, and stuffing his belt with his machete.

"You need to go with him, Zeek!" Jillian shoves him with teary eyes. He glares at her. "Of course I'm fucking going," he snaps at her. "I just want everyone to have a clear fucking head. We don't know what we're walking into," he informs, obviously the more level-headed one right now.

Jillian steps in front of me, and just as I'm about to push her out of my way she grabs my cut with force. Her blond hair falling in her face as she stares at me with wide eyes.

"Bring her back. Alive!" she cries.

ALESSANDRA

Finding rusting metal stairs, I take them one at a time. I feel confused, lost, out of my body as I find the door at the top. Using my shoulder, I push it over and the desert wind kicks up my matted hair. My side is bleeding and burning from the ripped stitches, wrestling with Black Hat they must have torn.

Climbing out I see Raven just ahead walking into the desert as if she is just as lost as I am. Where do we belong? Where do we go from here?

"Raven!" I scream, but she doesn't stop. She just continues to walk in a haze.

Wind slips past the bloody material of my uniform, and I feel misplaced wearing it. I don't deserve it. I am not a cop. My family is not real, my life was not real. Everything was a lie, a façade of what I really was. I wasn't living until just now.

I kick my boots off, as I walk into the night. I unbutton my pants and then my shirt. Letting the desert take them. Leaving my badge behind, my scuffed honor in the dust. The familiar roar of motorcycles sound just ahead, and my heart picks up its rhythm.

The Sin City Outlaws.

Standing there in a bloody white bra and red panties, Felix drops his bike and runs to me.

"What the fuck? Are you okay?" he asks with excitement and fear. I open my mouth to respond, but I shut it just as quickly and point at Raven who is walking into the desert. He looks over his shoulder in the direction of my hand.

"Machete, get her!" he orders and a bunch of guys go running after Raven.

"What the fuck happened, Black Bird?" He shakes out of his cut and places it over my shoulders, trying to conceal some of my bare body.

"I found out who I was. Who I am," I explain in a haze. The things I've done, the pain I've caused others. I think I even killed a kid the same age as me.

Grabbing my face, he makes me stare him in the eyes.

"You're mine, and that's all you need to fucking know," he snaps. He fully comes into view, everything else starting to dissipate as I take in what he just said. I'm his.

I'm not Brown 5. I have a home. I just had to relive my nightmare to realize it was with the Outlaws.

Felix

Lying in bed, I watch Alessandra stare at the wall. My body against hers she won't let me up to even piss. I saw what she did to that man in that fucking dungeon, and it scares me to see what exactly she is capable of. This is why I didn't want to tell her about her past, look at her. She is fucking lost, her demons battling the light inside of her. She doesn't know where to go from here, and I don't know how to help. I've accepted my hell, my life. She hasn't.

I wanted to rip the badge from her chest when I met her, but seeing her like this makes me glad it wasn't me who did that.

"Alessandra, talk to me," I tell her. She rolls over, looking at me with sad eyes.

"Where do I go from here?" she whispers.

"Wherever you want," I shrug.

"I'm a bad person. I did bad things," she mutters, running the nail of her finger along my collarbone. Her tone emotionless; numb.

"Then we have more in common than before." I cup her hand, and her eyes flick to mine.

"You don't know this new me. What I'm capable of." She shakes her head rolling onto her stomach. "What I've always been capable of."

My eyes fall on her scar of X, the one that Cross branded her with no doubt. She can always get a tattoo if she wants, it will cover it up. But if I know her like I think I do, she won't cover it up. She'll keep it as a reminder of what she's been through.

Running my finger along it I inhale a deep breath.

"Scars and memories remind us where we've been, babe, but they don't dictate where we're going," I tell her. It's something Carola has told me on my darkest days.

"I've always been on the side of the convicts then the side of the law. I've shot suspects and liked the way it made me feel; powerful. When I smell blood, I can't help but inhale it like someone would a bouquet of flowers, rather than look away in disgust. I never knew why, but I do now," she sobs, her voice cracking with raw emotions. Watching a girl become a woman right before me is something that no man can describe. The fairy tale her father sold her dimensioning to reality. It's breathtaking, majestic, and makes me fucking want to own her every breath and beat of her heart.

Her eyes search mine, a moment of silence speaking louder than anything we have to say to each other.

"I'm here no matter what, Alessandra. You could have devil horns or a halo and I'd be behind you with a smoking magnum ready to clear the path for you," I tell her, and it's true.

"I don't love you," she whispers with watery eyes.

Pulling her close I rest my head against hers. "I don't love you either."

She looks lost, like she's at a crossroad of what to do with her life. Does she live as an outlaw, or be a cop. I think she is both and needs to excel in both. It's what draws me to her in the worst way.

"Go back to being a cop." I can't believe I just said that. She flinches at my words.

"You hate cops?" She tilts her head to the side. I did say that, but that was before I saw who she really was, what she could do.

"The streets need you. Too often have cops have forgotten what it is like to be lost in the throes of poverty trying to survive. You gave Bishop another chance at life, anyone else would have locked him away. You think with your heart, and not the badge," I explain.

Alessandra turns her head looking at me with soft eyes, my words breaking through her wall of conflict.

She cups my cheeks, her cracked bleeding lips brushing against mine.

"What if my heart is black?"

"That's why I love you," I laugh and her eyes widen just as mine do when I realize what I just said. I can't take it back, so I just smirk. Grasping her hand, I pull it close, the smell of her sweet skin making my chest tighten. "I admit. My feelings for you started with hate, then I just wanted to fuck you. But then I got greedy and wanted your love, Alessandra," I tell her honestly.

"You can have all of me," her voice breathy.

"I plan to," I state, tucking a hair behind her ear.

"This ride could get me killed." She rubs her thumb along my bottom lip. I'm not sure what ride she's talking about. The one with me, or her going back to the department, but either way. I'll be by her side. I may not be a man that you can take home to Mom, a man of many words, and I have a temper that would scare any normal woman away. But Alessandra is mine, and she's crazy if she thinks I'm going anywhere else.

"Than society better make two graves because we're riding to hell together."

"The papers will say 'Bonnie and Clyde who?'" I smile like the devil.

ALESSANDRA

Taking a deep breath, I climb the steps to the station, my badge clasped in my sweaty hand.

Machete grabbed it and my gun from the desert that night, said he was keeping them company until I decided what I was going to do. But Mac told me he was fucking a chick wearing the badge and my gun on his hip one night. Wouldn't surprise me, so I made sure to sanitize both. That man is an animal, God knows what he did with them.

Entering the station, I keep my eyes focused on my target, the chief's office. I don't say hi to anyone, and I don't swipe a donut off the counter because it might make me second-guess what I'm doing here. I know what I'm doing and can't back out. This has to be done.

I head straight to the chief's office, scents of rose perfume strong, and toss the badge and my gun on her desk.

"What is this?" Chief Lopez asks, raising a brow at me. Her hair is in a perfect bun, her makeup flawless and light. She sighs, sitting back in her leather high-back chair with a resting bitch face.

"I quit. I'm not meant to be a cop," I shake my head, my lips twisted.

"Alessandra, don't do this. Your father—"

"I'm not my father, not even close. He was a good man and wanted me to do good things, but that just it. I'm not a good person, and I don't belong here. I've purposely broken rules, and you've looked the other way because let's be honest, you had respect for my father, not me," I cut the shit, and this catches her attention quickly.

She drops her bitch face and sighs heavily. The exhale of breath telling me everything she isn't saying. That I'm making a mistake, that any route I might be perusing is wrong.

"Are you sure this is what you want?" Her eyes cut to mine, they're so cold and unfriendly it makes me wonder how she ever gets laid.

A motorcycle just outside the window revs its engine, catching her attention. It's my ride, Felix. I can't help the way I light up seeing him, and Chief Lopez notices. She scoffs clicking her tongue with heavy judgment.

"You're making a mistake. This is crazy," she sneers, crossing her arms. Maybe, but I can't honor the code of blue, but I respect it.

"Maybe, but being normal is boring." I smile, lift my chin and start backing toward the door. I've said what I needed.

"I'll see you on the other side of the bars?" she asks arrogantly. Tapping my fingers on the doorframe I smile wolfishly.

"Good luck catching me," I wink, taking a step out of her office. Shit, I almost forgot. "Oh, and Raven told me to tell you she won't be returning to work either," I inform casually.

She scoffs, shaking her head like she's not surprised.

Heading outside, the summer sun hits my face just right. A weight I never knew lifted from my shoulders. I feel lighter, happier, and free. Walking out of the station without my badge my black wings were finally able to release themselves in full form. No more façade of something I was never meant to be. I tried to be a good person, live like a normal female, but I never felt like I fit. Let's face it, I've been through a lot of shit, and it got to me no matter how much effort my dad put into me forgetting it. It was always there, waiting to be released.

Felix is on his motorcycle smoking a cigarette when I approach, and God, I just want to pull his hair and fuck him on the back of it. Zeek and the rest of the men straddling their bikes right beside him. It's a circle of metal, leather, and trouble. Rugged men and angry stares looking about. Not too long ago I'd be nervous walking up to them, but now I feel safer.

"How'd it go?" Felix asks.

"They may hate us together, but they can't stop us," I shrug.

"That's a good motto!" Machete points at me, his red hair shining amongst the sun.

The way Felix's lips pull into a smirk has me holding my breath, and my heart beats a little faster.

He bends over pulling something from his saddlebag.

"I figured since you traded your badge in, it was time to properly make you my ol' lady," he states, holding up a cut that shows the club's colors and me as his ol' lady.

I cup my mouth, my eyes wide. I know what this means to him, to any woman of the club. The men go wild catcalling and clapping, making me feel welcomed more than I ever did joining the department.

"Taking this you fully accept my fucked-upness," he laughs.

"That's no shit!" Mac laughs, sitting in front of us smoking a cigarette.

Grasping the warm leather in my hands, I smell it, my eyes

closed. The tones of a free life, and chaos wafting around me.

"You giving this to me, you have to promise to see me as me and not a cop," I whisper. "All of you?" My eyes look around at the men and I get solid nods from them all.

"I never saw you as one anyway, otherwise I wouldn't have fallen for you," Felix says seriously. We'll agree to disagree on that one.

Opening my eyes, I slide my arms into the cut, and instantly feel like I found my place, that spot I've been looking for my whole life. My mom is welcomed at the club, even if she thinks Mac is my dad every other day. I'm welcomed in the club, and though Jillian was sent off to a safe-house, I get to talk to her on a burner phone on occasion. Carola is with her, and Zeek comes and goes protecting his club, and his woman.

I'm an outlaw, I just never knew it.

"Through the good and the bad, I'll ride or die, baby." I raise a brow, my lips pursed.

"That's my girl," Felix winks, smacking my ass before pulling me closer and laying his lips on mine. I cup his cheeks, his beard soft beneath my fingers.

Pulling always, I throw my leg over the seat and hold on to my man as he revs the motor. Citizens stare at us. Some whispering to their friends, others walking as fast as they can in the other direction.

"Let's ride!" he hollers, flicking his cigarette to the side.

Acknowledgements & Author Note

Oh man I missed the rush of writing the Nevada boys so much!

Felix and Alessandra surprised me with their story, that is for sure. I thought Alessandra would be more like a Barbie with a gun, and I was very wrong! What did you think?

And Machete... where the hell did that animal come from? I am jumping in his story now as I can't wait to see what comes from him! It's going to be crazy, I know that!

I want to thank my beta's for helping me through my writing blocks and smoothing out my work. Brie, Natalie, and Lindsey!

Thank you to my amazing editor Ellie, and my proof reader Kim for the final touches!

A big thank you to Allan Speirs! I had a vision for my cover and he helped me hit that target with that sexy man beast, and Sara Eirew nailed the cover with it!

The Rock Stars Of Romance - You rock as usual!

Big thank you to the blogs that have taken time to read my work and share it, that have supported my work and encouraged me. I can't thank you enough for what you do!

The readers, I FUCKING LOVE YOU! You make my dreams come true, and make writing worth banging my head against the keyboard to bring you my very best!

My husband listened to many snippets of this book and helped me, and my mom read this book twice to help me work the kinks. They are real troopers, and as awkward as it was for my mother to read it… she was a boss!

My Little Devils Street team, you've been my backbone and a place I run to daily to share my work in progress, and bits of my crazy life.

All of you are my team, my village, and I couldn't do this without you!

About the Author

M.N. Forgy was raised in Missouri where she still lives with her family. She's a soccer mom by day and a saucy writer by night.

M.N. Forgy started writing at a young age but never took it seriously until years later, as a stay-at-home mom, she opened her laptop and started writing again. As a role model for her children, she felt she couldn't live with the "what if" anymore and finally took a chance on her character's story.

So, with her glass of wine in hand and a stray Barbie sharing her seat, she continues to create and please her fans.

ALSO BY M. N. FORGY

THE DEVIL'S DUST SERIES

What Doesn't Destroy Us
(The Devil's Dust #1)

The Scars That Define Us
(The Devil's Dust #2)

The Broken Pieces Of Us
(A Devil's Dust Novella)

The Fear That Divides Us
(The Devil's Dust #3)

Love That Defies Us
(A Devil's Dust Novella)

The Lies Between Us
(The Devil's Dust #4)

What Might Kill Us
(The Devil's Dust #5)

SIN CITY OUTLAWS SERIES

Reign
(Sin City Outlaws #1)

Mercy
(Sin City Outlaws #2)

Retaliate
(Sin City Outlaws #3)

STANDALONE

Relinquish

Love Tap

WRITING AS MISSY BLAKE

Plus One

Website:
www.mnforgy.com

Goodreads:
www.goodreads.com/author/show/8110729.M_N_Forgy

Facebook:
www.facebook.com/pages/M-N-Forgy/625362330873655

Twitter:
twitter.com/M_N_FORGY

Newsletter:
www.mnforgy.com/newsletter/

M.N. Forgy's Reader Addicts Group:
www.facebook.com/groups/480379925434507/

Made in the USA
Columbia, SC
25 August 2018